HIMALAYAN HAZARD

Pet Whisperer P.I.

MOLLY FITZ

Editor: Jennifer Lopez (No, seriously!)

Cover & Graphics Designer: Cover Affairs

Proofreader: Tabitha Kocsis & Alice Shepherd

Sweet Promise Press
PO Box 72
Brighton, MI 48116

ABOUT THIS BOOK

Ever feel like your entire world has been turned on its head? That's how I've felt ever since the gang and I found out that Nan has been keeping major family secrets stashed neatly away in the attic.

What's worse, we still don't know exactly what happened, and I have so many follow-up questions, like is she still the same woman I always assumed she was? And can I ever fully trust her again?

With Nan unable to give me a straight answer, I invite my parents to join me for a cross-country train trip so that we can all discover the truth, once and for all.

Octo-Cat hitches a ride with us, too, and it's a good thing he does, because it isn't long before a dead body joins us in the dining car. Now we have two mysteries to solve, and fast —our lives and legacy depend on it.

AUTHOR'S NOTE

Hey, new reader friend!

Welcome to the crazy inner workings of my brain. I hope you'll find it a fun and exciting place to be.

If you love animals as much as I do, then I'm pretty sure you're going to enjoy the journey ahead.

Himalayan Hazard is just one of my many brain-tickling adventures! Many more will be coming soon, so make sure you sign up for my newsletter or download my app to help you stay in the know. Doing so also unlocks adorable pictures of my own personal feline overlord, Schrödinger, deleted scenes from my books, bonus giveaways, and other cool things that are just for my inner circle of readers.

You can download my free app here:
mollymysteries.com/app

Or sign up for my newsletter here:
mollymysteries.com/subscribe

If you're ready to dive right in to more Pet Whisperer P.I., then you can even order the next books right now by clicking below:

Hoppy Holiday Homicide
Retriever Ransom
Lawless Litter
Legal Seagull

And make sure you've also read the books that come before ***Himalayan Hazard*** in the series. They can be read in any order, but you'll enjoy yourself more if you start at the beginning!

Kitty Confidential
Terrier Transgressions

Hairless Harassment
Dog-Eared Delinquent
The Cat Caper
Chihuahua Conspiracy
Raccoon Racketeer

And don't miss these special collections!

Pet Whisperer P.I. Books 1-3
Six Merry Little Murders

Okay, ready to talk to some animals and solve some mysteries?

Let's do this!
Molly Fitz

To anyone who wishes she could talk to her animal best friend…

Well, what's stopping you?

CHAPTER ONE

My name's Angie Russo, and lately my life has taken one dramatic turn after another. Seriously, where can I even begin?

I guess it all starts with my cat.

Think that sounds boring? Well, think again!

My cat can talk. Only to me, but still.

We met at the law firm where I used to work as a paralegal. I never really loved that job, but I did enjoy having food in my fridge and a roof over my head, so I stayed despite being treated like a glorified secretary and not the shrewd researcher I'd worked so hard to become.

We had a will reading scheduled one morning, and I was called in to make some coffee for the attendees. The machine we had was approximately a million years old and unpredictable even on its best day. This was not one of its best days. All I wanted to do was make the cruddy coffee and get back to work, but—lo and behold—I got electrocuted and knocked unconscious instead.

And when I awoke from that zap, I found a striped cat sitting on my chest and making some pretty mean jokes at my expense. Well, as soon as I realized the voice was coming from him and he realized that I could understand what he said, that cat recruited me to help solve the murder of his late owner.

That's how I and Octavius Maxwell Ricardo Edmund Frederick Fulton Russo, Esq., P.I. became an item. I've since shortened his name to Octo-Cat and have become his official owner—although he'd surely tell you that he's the one who owns me, and, well... he wouldn't exactly be wrong.

He came into my life first with a murder mystery and then with a generous trust fund and even more generous list of demands. So now here we are, living in the posh manor house that previously belonged to his late owner, drinking chilled Evian out of Lenox teacups, and operating the area's best—and only—private investigation firm.

There was a brief upset when a raccoon named Pringle set up a competing business, but we've moved past that now. Because, yeah, at first I could only talk to Octo-Cat, but with time, I also gained the ability to communicate with other animals, too.

The regular cast of mammalian characters that make up my life include an eternally optimistic rescue Chihuahua named Paisley, that infamous raccoon racketeer named Pringle—also known as the Master Secret Keeper for our firm—an easily distracted, nut-obsessed squirrel named Maple, and my crazy-daisy, live-in grandmother, Nan.

Frankly, I'd love to add a bird to our merry little gang of forest misfits, but they're all too frightened to talk to either me or Octo-Cat. Go figure.

And despite our diverse skill set, our P.I. outfit isn't exactly successful. We've only had one case to date, and we weren't even paid for it. I know it will happen for us eventually if we just stay the course and continue to believe in ourselves…

Um, right?

Well, that's what Paisley insists, anyway.

Even still, I've got this huge new thing in my life that is keeping us plenty busy, with or without work to fill our days. I just discovered that I have a whole big family in Larkhaven, Georgia, that I never even knew existed until a couple weeks ago. And what's more, they've invited me, my mom, and dad to come down for an extended visit so that we can all get to know each other.

Octo-Cat insists on coming, too. He hates long car rides and refuses to even consider getting on a plane, which means we get to take the train. Whoopee.

Sure, it won't cost very much, but it will take longer than a day of continuous travel to get there. Still, I can't exactly leave him behind when he was a big part of helping me locate the hidden branch of our family.

Yeah, Nan had kept them hidden from us for my entire life and my mom's whole life, too. But now that we've found them again, there's no keeping us apart. Nan doesn't want to join us, even though Mom and I both assured her she'd be welcome. She still feels guilty about what happened.

Maybe we can convince her to join us for the next visit. I hope we can, because even though she kept a major secret from me, she's still my best friend and my very favorite person in the whole wide world.

That's why saying goodbye to her right now is so difficult…

"Promise me you'll call every single day," I moaned, hugging my grandmother so tight I had to wonder if she could even breathe.

"Mommy, I'm going to miss you, too!" Paisley, Nan's five-pound tricolor Chihuahua, cried as she pranced on the platform from the other end of her neon pink leash.

I scooped her up and peppered her adorable little face with kisses. "I'm going to miss you, too," I cooed in a cutesy, crazy pet lady voice. Talking to the animals like this in public made people think I was weird but kept my secret ability hidden. "Mommy will be back in sixteen days. You can wait sixteen days, can't you?"

"I don't know how to count," Paisley said with a happy bark.

I handed her over to Nan and took Octo-Cat's cat carrier from my mom so she could get in goodbye hugs, too.

My cat growled during the handoff. "Hey, there's delicate cargo in here!"

Mom and Nan said a quick goodbye, and then I set Octo-Cat down to hug her again. As pathetic as it might be to admit, I'd never been away from her so long. I'd grown up under her roof and lived with her most of my adult life, too—although now she lived with me rather than the other way around.

Throngs of passengers dragging big wheeled suitcases passed us on either side, and I had to step back to avoid getting hit by a fast-walking woman who was more focused on her phone conversation than where she was going.

"Look," I told Octo-Cat. "She has a cat carrier, too."

And she did. Only it was much fancier. I wouldn't be surprised if the bling adorning the case was actual diamonds—or at least Swarovski crystals.

"Show-off," my cat muttered, even though I'm pretty sure he'd have loved a decked-out carrier like that to call his own. It didn't matter that he'd sooner surrender one of his few remaining lives than willingly get inside.

"I'm surprised there are so many people out here," my dad said, glancing around uncomfortably. "I didn't realize anyone still took trains when there are so many other options available."

"It's romantic," my mom gushed, leaning into him and possibly squeezing his butt from behind. It seriously grossed me out how in love these two were, even after thirty years of marriage. They sure acted like high schoolers, sometimes.

"I feel like I'm about to rush platform nine and three quarters at King's Cross for the first time," I said with a snort and a chuckle.

"When were you at King's Cross?" my dad asked with a furrowed brow.

Ah, jeez. Sometimes it was hard being the only avid reader in the family. Had my parents seriously not even seen the movies?

"That's it!" I cried. "We've got like thirty hours aboard that train. More than enough time for a Harry Potter movie marathon, and when we get home, I'm lending you my book collection so that we can get you all the way caught up."

"Homework?" my mom whined.

"Ugh, you're the worst ever, Mom," my dad added.

And then they kissed so long and hard that my mom's foot popped up like a fairytale princess getting her first big kiss. Only this was their six millionth big kiss at least.

This was going to be a very long trip. Very long, indeed.

"The conductor's waving you over," Nan said, pointing toward a uniformed man standing just outside of our train car. "Best get a move on."

"Are you ready?" I asked Octo-Cat.

"Just get me out of this thing," he grumbled, as if this whole method of travel hadn't been his idea.

"Relax," I murmured as we made our way over to the step up into the train. "I'll have you out in two minutes, and then it will be smooth sailing from there. After all, what's the worst thing that can happen on a train?"

Famous last words… I really should have known better.

CHAPTER TWO

After giving Nan one last squeeze, the four of us strode up to the train and climbed aboard. Well, Octo-Cat was carried in what he'd deemed his "travel prison." In the back of the car, I found a grouping of four seats that faced each other, two on each side, and placed Octo-Cat's carrier onto the aisle seat, taking the spot by the window for myself.

Nan stood exactly where we'd left her on the platform, waving furiously and hopping up and down. "Bon voyage, my dear!"

I laughed and blew her kiss.

"You're just as embarrassing as she is," my mom muttered, scooching over in her seat so that she and my dad had not a millimeter of space between them. "No wonder the two of you are always conspiring on something."

I let that one slide, despite the fact that she and Dad were way more embarrassing than Nan and I would ever be. Mom had always felt sensitive about how close me and my grandmother were, and I knew she felt left out somehow. It was even worse now that we'd recently found out Nan wasn't her real mother, that she had in fact actively kept her from her birth mom based on the request of the man both women had once loved.

Yeah, we were still untangling that one…

That's why we were headed down to Larkhaven, Georgia. My grandfather's side of the family still lived down there and had invited us to come on over for a little family reunion. Of course, we had no idea where my biological grandmother had gone, or even if she was still alive. But one thing at a time.

My dad whispered something in Mom's ear, and she giggled.

"Gag me on my own hairball," Octo-Cat drolled beside me. My sentiments exactly.

Passengers continued to pile onto the

train. Dull chatter settled around me like a comforting blanket. Perhaps, this wouldn't be so bad, after all. I watched a mother with two young children settle near the front of the train, then an elderly couple settle a bit closer to us. All kinds of people chose trains over planes, it seemed.

Who'd have ever guessed that the rail travel industry would still be going strong in the twenty-first century? Not me.

A man wearing an old-fashioned fedora and argyle sweater vest slid into the seat across the aisle, then immediately withdrew a rickety looking typewriter and began to pound on the keys. His fingers moved deftly as he added word after word to the sheaf of paper hanging from the top of his old-fashioned machine.

A typewriter on a train. Two anachronisms in one.

Throw in the fedora, and that makes three.

Suddenly the man stopped typing and pushed his glasses farther up his nose as he turned toward me. "What's a good word for suspicious? Except for more subtle?" His unblinking eyes bored into me as he waited for some kind of genius revelation to spring forth from my mouth.

"Um, odd? Curious?" Kind of like you.

He rubbed his chin. "Hmm, I'm not sure those will work. Ahh, well. I'll come back to it in the second draft."

"The second draft? Are you writing a novel?"

That was kind of cool. My nan had always claimed she'd write a book, and little by little she had made progress over the past several months—although the book she was working on was a memoir, not a work of fiction. I often wondered if she planned to include the truth about my grandfather and bio-grandma.

"Oh, yes," the man said with a smile that lit up his whole face. "Not just any novel, the next great American novel. You see, it's about—"

"Angela!" Octo-Cat cried from inside his carrier, practically panting in his sudden onset of panic. "Get out! Get out now, or we will be forced to spend the entire journey listening to this guy's delusions of literary grandeur."

"It sounds wonderful," I told the aspiring novelist. "Unfortunately, my cat needs to be fed now."

The tabby yowled pitifully to help sell our story.

I still thought it might be cool to talk to a real live writer, but the fact that this one referred to his unfinished manuscript as the next great American novel was a flashing warning sign. This guy thought he was important, talented, God's gift to readers, even. I was all for credit where credit was due but believed it was better to let others sing your praises than to belt them out on your own.

"I'll be back later, okay?" I offered with a friendly smile. I didn't want to be unsupportive of his dreams, especially since my dream of becoming a full-time P.I. with my talking cat as a partner was every bit as crazy.

"And run," Octo-Cat directed.

I was not going to run away from the poor guy. At least not literally.

I stuck a Bluetooth device in my ear as we pushed through our car into the next. The thing hadn't worked in years, but it did provide a great misdirect when I felt the need to talk to Octo-Cat in a public place.

"What do you think?" I asked him as I felt the train jolt to life under my feet. My hand stretched toward the wall, catching me just in time to avoid my stumbling forward.

"Well, that was unpleasant" my cat complained with a low growl. "Can I please get out of this thing now?"

"I'll let you out as soon as we settle somewhere," I promised, pausing for a moment to glance out the window as we rolled away from the station. Nan was still out there waving like mad, but soon she became a speck on the horizon.

He sighed and thumped around in the case. "I know it was just an excuse to get away from Chatty McMyNovel, but I could use a meal or at least a spot of Evian."

"The dining car it is." I raised him higher and hugged the carrier to my chest as I pushed into the next car.

I hoped the conductor wouldn't give my parents a hard time for me being up and out of my seat already, but then again most of what I knew about trains came from old timey books and movies. Things seemed to run a bit different in our modern age of digitization.

Luckily, we only had to pass through three other passenger cars before reaching our destination. That was good news for the journey ahead. I liked knowing that snacks were nearby, should we need them.

"I should probably text Mom and Dad to let them know where we went." I unlatched the wire front door, and Octo-Cat sprang out onto the table twitching mightily.

"You do realize that in cat years that was almost a full prison sentence, right?" He shuddered, then plopped on his side and began to lick his kitty bits for all to see—and on an eating surface, no less. At least I was used to his less than courteous ways.

Shaking my head, I sent a quick text to my mom, asking if she needed anything while we were over here. As soon as I sent the message, my phone spat out a message to let me know I had a low battery. Twenty percent. Ugh, leave it to me to be so preoccupied with the upcoming journey that I forgot essentials like making sure I had a fully charged phone.

Glancing around the dining car, however, put my fears to rest. Every single table had an electrical outlet. I just needed to fine my phone charger inside my jumbled mess of a suitcase and then we'd be perfectly fine.

"I'll go see if they have any Evian," I told Octo-Cat.

He mumbled something, not bothering to pause his public ministrations to address me properly.

I sighed and shook my head again, then approached the snack station with a rumbling belly. Another basic necessity I'd ignored in my excitement over the trip.

The worker saw me approaching and forced a smile. His curly red hair fell forward into his eyes, and he reached up to brush it from his face. Perhaps I would stick to prepackaged food unless I was certain he wouldn't be the one preparing it.

I'd seen steak among the meal options, and that sounded really good right about now. Was it too early to order my dinner? I hoped not.

Before I could reach the counter to order anything, however, a woman wearing a cream skirt and matching peplum blouse intercepted me.

"Hello, there," she said with a friendly but placid grin. "Were you just talking with your cat over there?"

She glanced over my shoulder and nodded to Octo-Cat back at our table, then set her eyes back on mine with a knowing expression, aka an expression that suggested she'd already figured out my closely guarded secret.

Five minutes aboard a train, and I'd already made a major misstep.

Uh-oh.

CHAPTER THREE

I took a giant step back, but the lady reached out and grabbed my wrist, chuckling softly as she did.

"I didn't mean to insult you. After all, I talk to my Grizabella constantly. Few people understand the special bond between a woman and her cat. Wouldn't you say?" She tilted her head to the side and widened her grin.

I nodded as relief washed over me. "My name's Angie, and he's Octo-Cat."

"I'm Rhonda Lou Ella Smith." She held out her hand, which hung limp from her wrist. Did she expect a shake or a kiss? Either way, I was afraid of hurting her with my strong grip, so I settled on a fist bump… which failed miserably.

Rhonda brushed her hands off, then folded them in front of her waist. "Yes, well. Care to join us at our table? Better you than someone else, after all." She laughed again, and the sound reminded me of a bird singing at first morning light. Everything about her reminded me of a bird, actually—from the delicate bone structure to the expensive and perfectly tailored outfit and flashy jewelry all the way to her dazzling platinum hair.

"Sure, let me just order our snacks first." I turned back toward the red-headed counter attendant and he dropped his hand from his mouth sheepishly. Gross. I bit my nails, too, but not while working food service.

"Oh, don't you worry about that. I have more than enough to share," Rhonda promised, then sashayed back toward her table, moving so gracefully I had to wonder if she'd escaped from a ballet or a circus trapeze act or something.

"Okay, then. Be right over." I smiled again just in case she turned back at the sound of my voice and skulked back to my table, completely baffled by the elegant woman's interest in me. Was it really so simple as her feeling a bond to me as a cat owner?

"Whatever you agreed to, I didn't," my cat told me, sitting up straight and wrapping his striped tail around himself. "I'm staying right here."

"Then I guess you won't be getting any Evian," I whispered, turning my back to him and counting to five under my breath.

"One of these days I'm calling the animal cruelty association on you," he said from behind me, then jumped from the table onto my shoulder.

"Ouch! Claws!" He'd never hitched a ride on me before, so I wasn't sure why he wanted to do it now—other than perhaps thinking it could be a fun new way to humiliate, and thus punish, me for forcing him to make nice with the other passengers.

"What a cute trick," Rhonda chirped, clapping her hands in delight as we approached.

"Tricks? Aren't those for old dogs? I am a cat, madame," Octo-Cat said to our new friend, although I'm sure she only heard his croaky, entitled meow.

"Don't bother speaking to her," a smooth, lyrical voice rose from the bench seat. "She never understands."

My eyes darted to the gorgeous long-haired cat with dark face, tail, and paws and striking blue eyes. Must be the previously mentioned Grizabella. There were cats, and then there were cats. Grizabella belonged to the latter classification. She looked like she could have stepped out of a textbook, so perfect was her coat, her stance, basically everything about her.

Octo-Cat stiffened on my shoulder, brushing his whiskers against my cheek as he craned to see the Himalayan better. "Pray, Angela. Do you also see an angel before us?"

An angel? What?

I tried to turn to look at him, but only got a face-full of striped tabby fur. Irritated, I pried him from my shoulder and set him onto the empty bench seat across from Rhonda.

He didn't even protest. He also didn't stop staring at the other cat for even a second. As soon as I set him down, he hopped onto the table, his quest for Evian apparently a thing of the past.

"Dear beautiful feline, it is an honor and a privilege to look upon you," he said, his amber eyes growing larger the longer they beheld her. Either he'd been spending too much time around Pringle, our resident raccoon and medieval knight enthusiast, or he'd discovered one of the fantasy channels on TV. Knowing him, either was equally likely.

"I think my cat likes yours," I told Rhonda with a chuckle. I'd never seen Octo-Cat try to flirt before, and I kind of wish I hadn't seen it now.

"Careful," the woman warned. "Grizabella doesn't much like other cats, or people, or anyone, really." She reached out to stroke the Himalayan's long fur, but a quick paw batted her away.

Talk about a cat after Octavius's own heart.

"I do not appreciate your attempts to flatter me, house cat," Grizabella hissed, then cuddled up to Rhonda's side. Talk about hot and cold. Octo-Cat also had pretty intense mood swings, but normally in the space of an hour rather than mere seconds.

And, normally, such a slight would send my tabby into a mad spiral of hurling insults and lashing claws, but not this time. "You misunderstand. I am part Maine Coon, the most ancient of American-born breeds, and I am at your service, beautiful Grizabella." He dipped his head closer to the table and folded his ears out to the side in a show of respect.

"I don't need your service. My human meets my needs just fine."

"Hard to get," Octo-Cat remarked with a jaunty laugh.

"No. Impossible to get," Grizabella corrected, her tail flicking on the bench seat beside her and beating against her owner.

"Nothing is impossible." Octo-Cat winked, then licked his paw. "I will find a way. After all, solving mysteries is my job. I own half of a private investigation firm, mind you."

Grizabella did appear mildly impressed by this but said nothing.

I figured it was time for me to chat with the other human, lest we raise suspicion about our special communication link. "What brings you on board the train today?" I asked Rhonda, doing my best to focus my full attention on her.

Rhonda fingered the gold pendant that hung down from the chain of pearls around her neck. The piece was enormous and quite stunning, given the intricacy of the design carved into it. A cluster of matching pearls sat proudly in the middle of the piece, creating a real treat for the eyes. The thing must have cost an absolute fortune. On the contrary, my nicest piece of jewelry was a delicate sterling silver chain with a paw print charm that Nan had given me on my last birthday.

Rhonda glanced out the window thoughtfully. "I prefer rail travel. It's better for Grizabella."

"We're headed for Georgia," I volunteered. "Is that where you're going?"

"Not this time. We'll probably get off before then." Odd that she didn't actually name her destination, but I decided not to press. Pressing was not the point of making small talk, after all.

"I don't think I've ever been on a train

before. Well, except maybe at the zoo." I laughed at my own non-joke.

Rhonda did not. "You'll like it. There's nothing quite like it."

"I can see that already."

She smiled again, then returned her attention to the window. Strange she was so insistent on having us join her when she didn't really seem to want to talk.

We fell silent. Both of us turned our attention toward the cats, who, much to Octo-Cat's chagrin, had still not made friends.

"Oh, dear Grizabella. I will do anything for you, even lay down one of my nine lives." He crept to the edge of the table and sat right in front of Rhonda, who cooed happily and stroked his fur.

"Not interested," Grizabella said, lifting her nose into the air.

Octo-Cat ignored the human and continued to beg the Himalayan for her love. "I could catch a mouse. Would you like a nice dead mouse?"

Grizabella growled and ran under the table to avoid my poor lovestruck bumpkin.

When I glanced back toward Rhonda, she

was chuckling into a cloth napkin. "That's my Grizabella for you. She doesn't much approve of other cats, and they don't approve of her."

I was just about to argue that Octo-Cat approved greatly of the Himalayan, but then Rhonda said, "It's why we make such a perfect pair."

What a strange thing to say. Was this the wealthy woman's way of saying she didn't approve of me—or that she thought I didn't approve of her? Why would it even matter? And, again, why had she insisted on having us join her?

I smiled but said nothing in response. Eventually, she moved on to tell me stories of Grizabella's many mundane adventures. Honestly, I kind of wished I'd stayed with the writer guy.

CHAPTER FOUR

Although Rhonda had promised to share her cache of snacks, she never once made an offer while we were sitting together. By the time Octo-Cat and I dismissed ourselves from her table, I was too embarrassed to remind her but also worried it would be too rude to purchase snacks right in front of her. My hopes rested on my parents now and the knowledge that my sports-obsessed dad almost always had a protein bar or bag of trail mix on him.

"Are you sure you can't stay and chat a little longer?" Rhonda asked when I stood to go.

She glanced out the window again and I

looked out, too. Clearly, we'd been sitting together for quite a while, because dusk had already begun to fall across the rolling landscape. No wonder I was starving!

"I'm sorry. I really need to get back to my parents," I said with a shrug, hating how childish it made me sound.

"That's wonderful that you're so close with your family. Very special, indeed," Rhonda said, stroking her cat absentmindedly as she watched me prepare to leave.

By some miracle, Octo-Cat returned to his carrier willingly and without complaint, presumably because Grizabella was watching. Man, if I'd known finding him a girlfriend would be the ultimate bargaining chip, I would have played matchmaker a long time ago.

"So," I mumbled as I carried him back through the three cars on the way to ours, my Bluetooth placed perfectly. "Do you always go gaga for Himalayans, or is there something special about Grizabella in particular?"

He sighed blissfully. "I've never been in love before tonight. It's like a whole new plane of consciousness has opened itself to me." It seemed his first crush had turned him into Shakespeare. I didn't blame Grizabella for finding his affections so wearisome.

I rolled my eyes. "Just remember, we're not on the train for that long and you probably won't see her after we get off at our station. Or actually, Rhonda said they'd be getting off first..." It took me a moment to make sure I had recalled that detail correctly since I had to wade through hours of cat stories to get back to the beginning of our conversation.

Suddenly, I felt very sorry for my poor kitty. Not only did he not stand a chance, but he'd probably never see his crush again. "Just don't get all heartbroken over this," I warned. "I hate to see you hurting."

"Love always finds a way, Angela," he said sagely. Although in this particular case, I had no idea how things would work out, considering the object of his affection actively disliked him.

Also they were cats. Could cats even fall in love? It seemed like maybe they could. I hoped one day Octo-Cat would find a lady who would return his romantic longings. I was also incredibly happy that he was fixed, given his complete lack of modesty when it came to… well, everything.

"Does this mean you'll be more accepting of me and Charles?" I asked, hoping that my feline's own brush with love might get him to stop referring to my boyfriend as UpChuck.

He said nothing, but a giant purr rolled up from the carrier in what I had to assume was the kitty version of humming blissfully while thinking of one's beloved. Wow. He really had it bad.

Speaking of having it bad, I returned to my seat only to find my parents wrapped even tighter around each other as they both stared at my mom's laptop with rapt attention.

"What are you guys watching?" I asked, noticing that they were sharing a single pair of earbuds.

"Harry Potter and the Deathly Hallows, Part Two," my mom answered without removing her eyes from the screen.

"Ugh, you guys! Why are you starting with the last one?"

"Well, we need to know it has a good ending before we invest in such a long series.

Don't we?" my father asked with one raised eyebrow.

Personally, I hated spoilers. They took away at least half the fun. At least my parents were giving it a try, though. I had to give them credit for that.

The aspiring writer I'd met before stopped typing and seemed to watch us from his peripheral vision. Was he waiting for an opening to tell me about his novel again?

Looked like I had a choice to make. I could either cuddle up with my already too cozy parents and pretend to watch the movie or I could go off exploring again. After the chat with Rhonda and Grizabella, I needed some alone time to recharge, which meant I had to get out of there before the conceited writer guy launched a second attempt at conversation.

"I just needed to grab my jacket," I said, hoisting the lightweight denim from the seat and draping it over my shoulders. "Oh, and before I go, do you have something I can eat?"

"As the Boy Scouts say, always be prepared." My dad picked up his travel bag and tossed a granola bar my way, still not removing his eyes from the movie. Well, at least they really seemed to like it.

"Thanks," I called over my shoulder, already making a getaway. We'd already found the dining car, and it was probably too soon to go back if I wanted to avoid a second get-together with Rhonda. Perhaps I could find the viewing car and hang out there for a while.

We passed through the three cars between our seats and the dining car, then four more to find the empty glass-sided carriage with seats arranged down the center to face the giant walls of windows on both sides. Only the very top of the ceiling was covered in metal, providing a panoramic view as far as my eyes could see, just so long as I didn't tilt my head up or down.

I set Octo-Cat's carrier on the ground and opened the latch. He pranced right up to the giant window, his movements soft and swaying despite his hatred of that carrier. A gentle rain had begun to patter on the glass, surrounding us in a peaceful dream-like bubble.

"I wish Grizabella was here to see this," he said with a longing I'd never heard from him before, not even when he spoke of his late owner, Ethel Fulton. The poor guy had it so, so bad.

"It is romantic," I said, cuddling into my jacket and scooching around in my seat until I found the most comfortable position.

We both watched the rain for some time, and beyond that, the rolling hillside of whichever state we were steaming through now. Probably still Maine, or perhaps we'd made it to New Hampshire or even Massachusetts by now. I'd almost drifted to sleep when Octo-Cat hopped up onto the seat beside me and then climbed onto my lap, a rare move from him, indeed.

"Are you worried about meeting your family for the first time?" he asked as he padded my lap with his front paws to increase the comfiness before settling down to relax. He almost never asked how I was feeling. Normally he just told me—yes, told me how I was feeling. I decided not to point that out and just enjoy his concern. After all, I really did need someone to talk to about this.

"It's weird," I admitted, pensively stroking the fur at his neck. "I always thought I knew who I was and where I came from, and then suddenly it's all wrong. And the weirdest part is that I never would have known if Pringle wasn't such a sticky-fingered snoop."

As much as the raccoon irritated me, I would forever have him to thank for finding and revealing the truth about my mother's—and consequently, my—heritage.

Octo-Cat purred in a way that told me he could only be thinking of his new lady love. He still appeared to be paying at least some of his attention to me, too, so I asked, "What would you do if you were in my shoes?"

"Shoes?" He huffed at the suggestion. "You're such a human."

I couldn't tell whether or not this was intended as an insult, so I kept mum. I was incredibly human, after all.

He stopped purring and crossed his forelegs in front of him. "It's different for cats. It doesn't really matter where you came from. Only that you turned out right."

Such a simple thought, but a nice one.

Sometimes I really liked his way of looking at things.

"Cats don't see their families again after we're taken away. I mean, I guess strays and alley cats might." He stopped to shudder at the thought. "But what happened with Nan and your mom, that's really normal for cats. We are born to our cat family but then taken away by our human family, and that's where we stay."

"So what are you saying?"

"Nan is your human, and she's a good one. Things could have been much worse."

He was right about that. Sometimes my cat was so smart, and other times he stared at the wall for no apparent reason. He was weird, all right, but luckily our weirds matched just perfectly.

And with that thought, I drifted off to the sound of his purrs.

CHAPTER FIVE

The continuous song of the rain and the unexpected bliss of kitty cuddles lulled me to sleep right where I sat. I dreamed I was Anne of Green Gables taking that first fated train ride that would deliver her to the Cuthberts. A nice dream, considering Anne was one of my all-time favorite heroines.

The lovely dream came to an abrupt end, however, when a horrible shriek rent the air and four sets of claws dug deep into my lap.

"Ouch, careful!" I cried, shooting to my feet so fast that Octo-Cat fell to the ground.

He immediately popped back to all four feet and stood with his tail drooping toward the ground and his neck stretching toward the roof. "It's my Grizabella!" he said, his ears twitching like satellite receptors. "She is in trouble. We must go to her."

The shriek shattered the night once more, and I realized then the scream was, in fact, feline and not human. That didn't make it less frightening, but it probably meant that most other passengers would choose to ignore it.

"It's this way," Octo-Cat cried, pouncing toward the door that led the opposite direction from whence we'd come. I assumed this led to the fancy sleeper cars, the ones we couldn't quite afford but that I had no doubt Rhonda Lou Ella Smith could.

My cat was too worked up now to stuff him back in his carrier, so I grabbed it and ran after him.

He stopped at the door and shouted, "I'm coming, my darling! I'm coming!"

The shriek sounded again. This time it was accompanied by the words, "Hurry!"

I had no idea what we were walking—or rather running—into, but it definitely sounded urgent. We passed through two sleeper cars, then opened the door to the third. When we entered, we found the wailing Himalayan pacing the hall.

She ran straight up to us and nuzzled Octo-Cat's face. "Thank you for coming so fast. My mistress… She—Oh, gosh. It's too horrible to even say!"

Octo-Cat appeared momentarily tongue-tied, so I took the lead.

"Can you show us?" I asked, holding my hand out to show her I meant no harm.

Grizabella took a quick sniff and then turned, her poofy tail held high while the rest of her quivered with fright.

The tabby and I followed her into one of the private rooms. The door was already cracked open, and inside our new friend Rhonda lay in a creeping puddle of blood, her flawless cream suit stained almost beyond recognition.

I brought both hands over my mouth to keep from crying aloud when I noticed one of the steak knives from the dining car sticking straight out of her stomach, where she had apparently been stabbed multiple times. But why hadn't she cried out? Surely, she would have screamed loud enough to awaken me from my dreams.

On shaky feet, I tiptoed across the soiled carpet, careful to avoid the encroaching red stain, and bent down to feel for a pulse. When I couldn't find one on Rhonda's wrist, I tried her neck, hoping beyond hope…

Her lovely pearl necklace with the gold pendant was gone. Had the murderer taken it? Did they kill this poor, kind woman just so they could rob her? The thought made me blindingly mad.

I shook my head as I turned back toward the cats. "I'm so sorry," I told the distraught Himalayan.

"Oh, why? Why?" she ground out. "Why musts humans only have one life? And why must Rhonda's have come to an end so suddenly?"

Oct-Cat pushed his face against hers, and the kindly nuzzle did appear to offer some comfort. Poor, poor Grizabella.

Even though she was still shrieking and asking various permutations of the question Why? I knew I needed to find out what she'd seen and if she had any idea who could have done this… and yes, why.

"C'mon. Let's go out into the hall," I said, not wanting to hang out around a dead body any longer than we had to. I made sure the door wasn't locked, and then shut it gently behind us. "Grizabella, did you see what happened?"

She shook her head and squeezed her blue eyes shut tight. "Only after. Not during."

"Where were you when she was attacked?" I pressed, already seeing she would be a difficult witness to question. It was to be expected for a cat, especially one in the throes of an emotional meltdown.

"I don't want to talk about it," she sniffed.

Well, that direct refusal raised more than one red flag. I'd investigated cats as possible suspects before. Would Grizabella prove to be the culprit in her owner's murder, too?

"Please," Octo-Cat chimed in, finding his voice acting the role of my partner once more. "We're here to get justice for your human, not to judge."

"Promise not to tell anyone?" Grizabella asked with a sad sniff.

"Of course we won't tell," I assured her, and not just because anyone else I talked to about this case would immediately dismiss me as a quack if I started sharing the cat's alibi.

"I was in the little kitty's room, using my box. I heard someone enter and speak with Mistress just as I was in the middle of... Well, you know. The sounds were muffled, I didn't know what she said. I waited in the other room until I heard the stranger leave, not wanting to have to play nice with any other humans for the night. No offense, but you were already more than enough for one evening." She turned toward me and crinkled her nose. Ugh, cats were so rude sometimes.

"Go on," Octo-Cat urged with a tenderness he never assumed when speaking with me. "What happened next?"

Grizabella gasped, remembering. "When I came out, Mistress was covered in blood and her skin had already started to turn cold."

I briefly wondered if I should pet the Himalayan to try to calm her down, but that didn't seem like the best idea, considering she'd barely tolerated her beloved human's touch.

"Wow, that's a lot to take in," I said instead. "If you don't mind, let me ask a few follow-up questions. First, didn't you hear Rhonda—I mean, Mistress—scream?"

"No, she did not scream or even sound upset." The set of her jaw and the firmness in her eyes told me she had no doubt about this.

"Okay. You referred to the stranger as a she. Does that mean the person who entered was a woman?"

"Oh, darling, I don't know. All humans look and sound the same to me." At least I'd been upgraded to darling, although I suspect she might use the same pet name for the help as well—well, if she could. She did seem to understand that I wanted to help and had begun to cooperate a bit better.

"That's what I always said, too," Octo-Cat said with a hum. "Until I got to know them a bit better."

"Yes, I did notice your human can talk," Grizabella said gracefully lowering herself into a sitting position. "Why is that? And don't you think it's just a tad suspicious?"

He shook his head, immediately coming to my defense. "She's here to help. We both are. Is there anything else you can tell us that might help us figure out what happened to your human?"

"Well, I know what happened. She's dead."

Great. We had a dead body that so far only I had discovered, and the only witness was a spoiled purebred who couldn't really tell us anything, anyway. This case would be almost impossible to solve before the train arrived at the next station and the proper authorities had a chance to take over. Should I still try, or should I quietly alert the staff and do my best to secure the scene until help arrived onboard?

Our train passed through a tunnel, turning the night sky even darker than before. I caught sight of heavy stone walls from the hall window and shuddered. It felt like we were passing through a tomb.

How fitting.

I pulled out my phone to check the time. Just past four in the morning. We didn't have any stops scheduled until seven thirty. Could we make it three and a half hours with a fresh corpse on board? And who should I tell given that the entire train seemed to be fast asleep?

The light flickered overhead and then blinked off with a startling pop. Oh, great, electrical problems were exactly what we needed now. Well, at least things couldn't get much worse, right?

This was always a bad question, whether or not I asked it aloud.

Because at that exact moment, the train grinded to a stop right in the middle of that dark, tomb-like tunnel. We were stuck in the countryside with a murderer—a violent murderer—on the loose, and I couldn't even see the hand in front of my face.

How very perfect.

CHAPTER SIX

I pulled out my phone to activate the flashlight. Sixteen percent battery life remained. I really needed to invest in one of those portable chargers in case I ever again found myself trapped on a dark train with a violent killer in the future.

You know, providing I survived this time…

A giant shudder racked my body as my phone chimed merrily into the silence. It's ringing!

Fumbling, I answered the call and raised the phone to my ear with shaking fingers. My mother's voice burst through the speaker.

"Angie! Where are you? Are you okay?"

"Mom," I cried. Normally, I was pretty cool under pressure, but this time I couldn't help it. Seeing Rhonda's butchered body up close and now being trapped in the dark right outside the door that led to her corpse, it was too much for me. It would be too much for anybody.

This wasn't my hometown. In fact, I didn't even know where we were on our journey from Maine to Georgia. I didn't know the other passengers and had no idea which of them might be a killer. There was no one to trust.

No one except my cat and my parents.

"What's wrong? Tell me how to get to you," my mom shouted into the phone, instantly sensing something was wrong and thankfully not forcing me to say anything more until she could first make sure I was safe.

"Past the dining car. Past the viewing car. In one of the private coaches. Hurry." I didn't have to tell her to bring Dad, because I knew she automatically would. Maybe between the three of us, we could straighten this mess out. Of course, there would be no way to save poor Rhonda Lou Ella Smith. Not anymore.

I sank to the ground against the wall and hugged my knees while waiting for my parents to make their way back to us. I'd be the calm, rational detective later. Right now, though, I needed a few minutes to feel my emotions so that I could work through them and let them go.

Something furry brushed against my arm in the darkness.

"Why are you crying?" Octo-Cat asked me curiously. "You don't cry."

"It's the dark. I think it's making everything so much worse," I sobbed while groping for him. As soon as my hand made contact with his fur, a bit of my bravery returned. We'd been through all kinds of dangerous scrapes before, but we'd always made it through. Together.

"The dark isn't so much different than light. Right?" He moved away, and I shivered from the sudden absence of his warmth.

"Maybe for a cat. Humans don't have night vision like you do." While I explained this, I was struck with an idea. The two cats were the only ones on the train who could see without the assistance of a flashlight, which meant they were the only two who could sneak around without attracting attention.

"Octavius, Grizabella," I called to them, not sure how close either was to me at the moment. "Can you two explore the train a little? See if you can find anyone suspicious?"

"What makes a human suspicious?" the Himalayan asked in her soft, melodic voice from across the dark car.

This was good. Focusing on the investigation helped to push the fear aside. Worry would only throw me off my game, and I needed all my wits about me, considering one of my senses had already been all but disabled.

"If they have blood on them for one. This person might also be sneaking around or searching for something. We still have no idea why someone would kill Rhonda, so until we figure that out, we need to look for general clues. Got it?"

"We can handle that," Octo-Cat assured me, his voice a bit deeper than normal, which I assumed was some part of his misguided flirtation efforts. "The only problem is we need a human to open the doors between cars."

Oh, right.

Just then, as if on cue, the door to our car opened, and my parents rushed in, their path illuminated by the sweeping of their twin phone lights.

"Turn one of those off," I hissed. "We need to conserve battery power. We have no idea how long we'll be stuck out here in the dark."

"Well, it's nice to see you, too," my mom scoffed.

I forced myself to my feet, keeping one hand on the wall to steady myself. "Mom, Dad. There's been a murder."

"What? When?" my dad demanded, surging forward and lowering himself to inspect me.

"Right before the lights went off and the train stopped."

My mom dropped to the floor, too, and hugged my head to her chest. "Oh, Angie. It's not safe for you to be back here on your own."

"Well, now you're here, so I'm fine. See?" I forced a smile, but Mom's light was focused elsewhere.

"I can't see much of anything at all," she grumbled.

I untangled myself from her arms and sat up higher. "Listen, Dad. Can you go find someone who works for the train company? Let them know we have a dead body back here and that it was definitely a murder. Call Mom if they need more details. My phone is almost dead."

"Sure," he answered, his voice sure, unafraid. "But what will you two do?"

"Do you even have to ask?" Mom said, and I could picture her with one hand on her hip and her eyes narrowed even though she still sat on the floor beside me.

"Solving the murder," he responded with a knowing chuckle. "Got it. Just be careful."

Mom pushed herself to her feet, leaving her light on the ground beside me. "You, too. I love you too much to lose you." After my mom said this, a sticky smacking noise filled the car. Of course.

"That goes double for you two," my dad

answered before switching his phone light back on and leaving me and my mom behind to take care of business.

"Wait!" I called just before the door latched closed behind him. "Follow him," I told the cats. "Dad, take it slow at the doors. The cats are going to follow you to see if they can find anyone acting suspiciously."

"Roger that." My dad probably saluted, but I couldn't quite see due to the angle of his light. My mother had told him about my strange ability long ago, but he'd never worked with me and Octo-Cat on a case before. I liked how he agreed to my request without arguing or questioning it.

"When he comes back, you two come back, too. Okay?" I told my cat.

Octo-Cat's brown-striped body moved into my dad's spotlight, and he turned back to regard me with a frown. "Angela, please," he hissed. "I've got this. Ladies first, Grizabella."

The Himalayan walked ahead confidently, tail and nose both held high. The door whooshed shut behind them, and they were gone.

"Show me the crime scene," Mom said,

not wasting even a single second. I may be the family P.I., but she was an ace reporter who loved solving mysteries, too. We'd only worked together a little before, but I sure was happy to have her on my side now.

The last of my tears having spilled, I pulled myself to my feet and directed Mom's hands—and thus her phone light—toward Rhonda's door. "In there," I whispered.

I kept my hand on hers, and we pushed the door open together. This time, I knew what we would find, which made it a bit easier to head back inside despite the pitch black that enveloped everything.

CHAPTER SEVEN

Mom led the way into our victim's private room. There lay Rhonda exactly as she'd been when I first discovered her less than half an hour ago. Poor soul.

"I'd say next time we should upgrade our travel plans," Mom said, shifting her light around the room and illuminating the cushy furnishings that I hadn't really gotten the chance to notice earlier. "But this isn't exactly a shining endorsement for first class."

"Can you shine the light on Rhonda's body?" I asked, ignoring Mom's ill-timed joke. "I want to see if there's anything I missed before." Because if I missed the entire room outside of her body, I probably missed some important clues, too.

"You knew her?" Mom asked, her voice quirking in surprise.

"We met in the dining car and talked for a little bit."

"How did that happen?" She found the light switch and flipped it back and forth, just in case. Nothing.

Having Mom here centered me. Not only was there safety in numbers, but she also might catch something that I would otherwise overlook. Together, we could do some good here—or at least keep things from getting worse.

"She asked me to sit with her and bond over our crazy cat ladiness," I admitted with a fond smile as I remembered how desperate she had been simply to make a new friend. "That Himalayan belongs to her, and Octo-Cat is quite smitten."

"He always did like the finer things," my mom said thoughtfully, then cleared her throat and focused her phone on Rhonda's body. "Did she tell you anything that might be relevant to her murder?"

I bit my lip as I studied Rhonda's face. Her features weren't distorted by terror or even anger. She simply looked at peace, which I found all the more unsettling. "We didn't say much, and I wasn't cataloging our conversation for later use, but at least one thing stood out. She either didn't know or wouldn't share her destination."

Mom flinched at this revelation, turning to face me with wide eyes. "What do you mean?"

"I told her we were going to Georgia, and she said she'd probably get off before then. Probably. Not definitely."

"So she had no clear destination in mind," she summed up.

"That's what I'm thinking. Or something happened to make her want to get off earlier than planned." She'd looked distracted and had glanced out the window an awful lot. Could that be related?

"Lot of good that did her." Mom swept the light down Rhonda's body and paused when she reached her stomach. "Stabbed multiple times. It looks like maybe five. It's hard to tell with all the blood."

I felt sick to my stomach, remembering how much I'd craved steak earlier that evening. Now I would probably never want to eat it again—or at least I'd be using a butter knife to saw off bite-sized pieces. "Someone had to have enough foresight to take the steak knife from the dining car, but the presence of multiple wounds makes me think this was a crime of passion."

"So, premeditated, but only very slightly. Hmm." Mom's carefully coifed hair didn't even move as she shook her head from side to side. Small wrinkles lined her forehead and the edges of her mouth, though, while she stared at the body pensively.

"Grizabella—that's her cat—said she heard Rhonda talking with someone after they entered the room. She was in the bathroom at the time and couldn't make out any of the words. She also couldn't tell if the visitor was male or female," I revealed, wanting to make sure she had just as much information as I did.

Mom sighed. "Meaning we don't have much to go on."

"Maybe the room has a clue. You have

the light, so maybe you can search her things while I see what I can find on her phone."

She turned on me so fast, I lost my breath from the sudden fright. "Why don't you have a light?"

"My phone is almost out of battery. Trying to conserve it in case there's an emergency later."

Mom sighed. "I'd tell you to be more responsible, but I'm guessing this is already one heck of a lesson. Let's find her phone so you can get started."

She shone her tiny flashlight around the room, locating Rhonda's cell phone almost immediately. It lay on the dresser beside a small travel case that looked like it would be used for makeup or toiletries. "I'll start here," Mom said, unzipping the case and riffling through the contents.

While she did that, I picked up the phone, praying it would be easy to access. And yes! Thankfully, Rhonda had elected to use a fingerprint to unlock her phone rather than a passcode, so I returned to her body, then very carefully and very respectfully pressed her index finger to the surface. The dark lock screen gave way to a photo of Grizabella sitting on a plump pillow and staring straight into the camera.

Aww. She really had loved her cat.

While that was sweet, however, it wouldn't help me figure out who killed her or why. I needed to learn more than just the surface stuff during our search, needed to find something that could set me and my mom on the right path.

So first I checked her email.

All the unread messages made me cringe. I'd always been an inbox clearer and couldn't understand people who hoarded thousands of unread messages, especially when so much of it appeared to be spam. After scrolling through the first several dozen emails and finding nothing but cat blogs and clothing sales, I decided to move on to her social media.

Unsurprisingly, Rhonda's Instagram was actually a fan account for Grizabella. She only had a couple thousand followers, but they appeared to interact regularly with her posts. I scrolled through the recent hearts and found almost every profile picture to be either a cat or a person smiling beside a cat. Well, Rhonda clearly had one very specific use for the platform—one and nothing else.

On Twitter, she followed a handful of politicians and other celebrities but didn't appear to tweet anything herself. Also not helpful.

But what would Facebook bring? Hopefully something a bit more useful.

Here, Rhonda had very few friends and posted rather infrequently. Her most recent update was a check-in at a train station in New Brunswick, which was strange because I was pretty sure I remembered seeing her on the platform when we'd boarded in Bangor.

Rhonda's post simply read: Off on another journey!

Scrolling through her feed revealed the usual combination of baby pics, wedding pics, and humble brags from her modest friends list. Hmm.

"Angie," my mom whispered. She hadn't been whispering before, so whatever she had to say, I was guessing it would be good. "I've found something."

I swung the phone around to illuminate

the room and found her sitting on the edge of the bed with her legs crossed at the ankle. In her hand, she held a small book, and on her face she wore an excited smile.

Here we go.

CHAPTER EIGHT

Like most older people I knew, Rhonda had kept her phone fully charged, which meant I didn't need to be careful about preserving its battery life—and thank goodness for that. I used the screen to illuminate my path as I moved carefully past her body and joined my mother at the bed.

"It's her personal planner," Mom revealed, flipping through the pages demonstratively. "You know, like the calendar app, but on paper."

"C'mon, Mom. I know what a personal planner is." The cover on this one was made of blue leather that I suspected matched the exact shade of Grizabella's eyes. Gold trimmed the edges of each page, not unlike a Bible.

Mom shook her head and continued to search through the entries until she landed on the current week. "Here," she pointed to the box reserved for yesterday. "She got on in New Brunswick. A bit earlier than us."

"I found the same thing on her Facebook profile, but I could've sworn we saw her when we were saying goodbye to Nan. She was in a hurry, but I definitely remember that blinged out cat carrier of hers."

Mom tucked her heavily hair sprayed hair behind her ears, but it immediately bounced back to its previous shape. "Huh. I don't remember seeing her, but maybe she just got off to stretch her legs."

"Or to a say a quick hello to someone waiting at the station," I suggested. We'd only seen her returning, though. Huh, indeed.

"So she got off, but she got back on," Mom recapped with a shrug. "Hang on. Let me see what else is in here."

While she thumbed through the planner, I returned to Rhonda's email and searched the name of the train company. Sure enough, since she never discarded anything, her travel itinerary popped right up.

"She was headed to Houston," I told Mom hardly believing anyone would want to be on a train for such a very long trip, but then again, maybe it wouldn't be so bad with a private room. Still, she had either knowingly lied to me or changed her plans quite suddenly. "She told me she'd probably get off before Georgia."

Mom stood and marched over to me, then shoved the planner in my free hand. "Her planner has a cat show in that area early next week."

So a sudden change of plans, then. "I wonder if the person she met at our stop said something that spooked her. Like maybe a threat. Maybe she reached out to me in the dining car because she felt safer with company."

Now I felt terrible. Had I been given the opportunity to save her, only to run away because I couldn't take another mundane cat story?

"That's a lot of maybes," Mom said, rubbing my shoulder like she somehow knew

I was partially blaming myself for poor Rhonda's fate. "I do agree this is all very suspicious, but we don't know anything for sure."

I shook those feelings aside and focused on the facts. Whether or not I'd played a role in what had happened, the best thing I could do now was to find justice for the poor lonely woman who loved her cat more than anything else in this world.

"She was wearing a necklace when I met her, but the necklace was gone when Octo-Cat and I came in presumably just minutes after her murder," I told Mom, forcing myself to move on.

Mom frowned and set the planner down where she'd initially found it. "Missing neck-lace. Quick visit to the platform in Bangor. Abandoned trip to Houston. Five stab wounds. We have a lot of little bits and pieces, but not enough to know what kind of puzzle we're building."

"Don't forget the distraught feline. It was Grizabella's cries that alerted us to the trou-ble." Despite the Himalayan's cool demeanor when we'd first met her in the dining car, her reaction to Rhonda's death showed the cat had loved her owner just as much as she'd been loved by her.

"Now that's interesting. Could it be a jealous cat show competitor?" Mom ventured, taking the planner back from me and holding it in both her hands as we continued to talk. "They were on their way to a show, after all. Maybe someone threatened them to keep them on the sidelines this year, so another cat could take the crown."

"I don't think cat shows work the same as beauty pageants," I said with a wry laugh. Laughing was good. It kept the horror from creeping in. "But it's not a bad theory. A jealous rival killed her off and then took the necklace to make it look like a simple robbery."

Mom nodded, but her face remained grim. "There are worse reasons to take a life. Not many, mind you, but I'm sure there are at least some."

The door swung open so suddenly, it made us both jump in fright. My heart hammered a heavy tattoo against my chest.

"Hellooooo!" a young male voice

bellowed. Then he gasped and his voice became higher. "Holy heck, so that guy's crazy claims are true, after all." He moved into the room and shone his lantern-style flashlight on Rhonda's body. The curly red hair immediately struck me as familiar. This was the same worker I'd spied in the snack car, the one I'd almost bought snacks from before Rhonda intercepted me.

"Hi. That crazy guy was my husband," Mom said, offering him a friendly wave.

The man—who couldn't have been much older than a teenager—staggered back and lifted a hand to his chest. "Yeesh, don't do that! I thought the dead was rising again."

Okay, so this kid had seen one too many zombie movies in his day. He also had access to the dining car and all of its knives. Could he be the killer returning to the scene of the crime? If so, Mom and I could definitely take him. Not that I wanted to engage in a fight to the death... now or ever.

"What are you doing in here?" I asked, studying him closely. His pale, blemished skin looked ghastly in the glow of his lantern. His skinny arms didn't appear strong enough to inflict the wounds I'd seen on Rhonda, but then again, young mothers could lift entire vehicles to save trapped babies—or so the rumor went.

"My boss sent me over here to check it out, since my station was the closest. He said that—" He stopped abruptly and raised his light higher. "Ha! Nice way to distract me. What are you doing in here alone with a dead body?"

He took another big leap back into the hall, terror washing over his once accusing features. "Wait. Did you kill her? Are you going to kill me?"

"Well, that depends…" Mom said and then moved slowly toward the frightened worker.

Yikes! What was happening?

CHAPTER NINE

"Mom," I shouted, at the same time elbowing her in the stomach.

"She's kidding," I assured the young train worker. He hadn't shown up at work today knowing he'd have a dead body and a crazy small-town news anchor to deal with, and Mom's attempt at humor was definitely not helping to ease the tension this time.

Mom said nothing, so I continued chatting nervously, even going so far as to raise my hands to show we meant the young man before us no harm. "We were the ones who discovered the body. Dad went to tell your boss while we stayed here to make sure no one would disturb the scene. You work in the dining car, right? I think I saw you there earlier. What's your name?"

He stepped back into the room, his shoulders sloped forward defensively or perhaps in defeat. "Yes, that's me. My name is Dan, and I'm just trying to do my job and—you know—not get murdered."

"Aren't we all?" Mom said, and I elbowed her in the ribs again.

"I'm Angie, and I'm a private investigator back in Maine. The deceased is Rhonda Lou Ella Smith. I met her earlier today. Perhaps you saw us together in the dining car."

Dan nodded, even chanced a smile. "Yeah. Yeah, I think I did."

Good. This was good. Now that he recognized me, he relaxed enough to hold a rational conversation and to stop accusing me and mom of murder.

"I'm trying to piece together what I can, so I can hand things over to the cops when they arrive," I continued, motioning toward the planner in mom's hands and then showing him the phone in mine. "Was she there a long time before I came in or a long time after I left? Did you notice anything unusual about her?"

Dan took the phone from me but didn't do anything with it other than hold it at his side. It seemed to further relax him, though. After all, most murderers wouldn't hand over evidence that could likely convict them.

"I don't know," he said after a slight pause. "She seemed normal enough. Weird, but normal."

"Weird how?" I pressed, keeping my eye on the phone. I would need that back at some point.

"She kept talking to her cat like it was a person. I noticed people looking at her funny, but I thought it was kind of nice. Who's to say cats can't understand us, right?"

"Sure," I said dismissively, happy Mom kept quiet on that one. While she thought revealing my secret pet-whispering ability would make for a great human-interest story, she at least respected that I'd prefer not to let the world in on my strange power. "Did you notice when she arrived in the dining car or when she left?"

"She came in right when we left the

Bangor station," Dan said, then nodded in confirmation. "I remember, because she was my first customer and it was just the two of us until you arrived a short while later."

"Did the two of you talk?"

"Just enough for her to place an order. It was a big one."

"Could you tell me if—?"

The door swung open again, and in marched my father. The two cats followed him inside, and then a fourth figure joined us in the private room. Dad shut off his phone—not needing it now that Dan was here with his lantern—then made his way to Mom's side.

The cats stayed quiet, watching us from near the doorway.

I couldn't quite make out who the new person was, given that the brim of his hat cast his face in creepy shadows. But then he opened his mouth to talk, leaving no doubt as to his identity.

"Wow," he said on the wings of a dramatic exhale. "You read about it. You write about it. But you never think you'll actually stumble upon a real-live murder mystery. And on a train. This is so Agatha Christie!"

"Easy, Tolstoy. There's been a murder here. Show some respect for those of us who didn't make it," my father warned, wrapping his arm around Mom's waist protectively.

"Who's this guy?" Dan asked, swinging his light closer to the writer who'd invited himself into this intimate scene.

"The name's Melvin Mann. Remember it, because one day soon you'll see it at the top of the New York Times Bestsellers list." I couldn't be sure given the current lighting situation, but I think he actually made jazz hands to punctuate his expression.

Oh, brother.

"Well, Melvin," I said slowly, trying not to gag on my words. "This is a crime scene, not Grand Central Station. I think it's time you went back to your seat."

"Oh, really? What gives you any more right to be here than I have?" He crossed his arms over his chest and stepped deeper into the room.

"Because I'm a P.I. That's why." Would I really need to establish that with each new person who arrived? Apparently.

He leaned forward, making himself several inches shorter so he could look me right in the eye. "Prove it." His words smacked of condescension. Not only did this guy think he was better than everyone else, but he also seemed to think I was worse. Infuriating.

"What? I can't prove it beyond my word."

He straightened back to full height. "Show me a business card or something." Right, because it was impossible to create cards that read anything you wanted them to.

Case in point, Melvin pulled a stack of cards out of his pocket with a flourish and handed them around. "See, Melvin Mann, novelist. Now show me yours?"

"I don't have any business cards on me. Sorry." I would have turned out my pants pockets, if I had any. He seemed the kind of guy to appreciate overwrought gestures, like purple prose in real life.

He jabbed a finger at me so hard it would

probably be a bruise. "Ah-ha! See, I knew you were just pretending."

My father rushed to my side and stared at Melvin so ferociously that the other man couldn't help but take a step back.

"Look, we can stand here arguing until the killer finds us, too," my dad said, not taking his hard eyes off the writer for a second. "Or we can work together to solve this thing."

"Oooh, I like that," Melvin said, steepling his fingers in a far too sinister fashion for my liking. "This is wonderful inspiration for the mystery story arc of my novel."

I held in a sigh, an eyeroll, and a groan all at once. "Earlier you were asking me about suspicious characters, so why don't you go find some?"

"I wasn't asking about the characters. I have my characters on lock, thank you very much. I was asking about synonyms."

"Just do what she says, JD Salinger," my father growled, taking another threatening step forward.

Melvin stood in place; a smile snaked

across his face. "You think calling me by classic novelists' names is an insult, but it's really quite the opposite."

Dad did not hold back the choice words he had in response to that.

I turned to Dan, ready to put this whole macho showdown—or whatever the heck it was—to rest. "Can you go check in with your bosses? See if we can get the train moving again or the police sent to our location. Something. Anything to help."

"Can do," he said, offering a thumbs up and a smile. At least he was more cooperative than Melvin Mann. The haughty writer would be a liability in this investigation, no doubt.

"Great. Thanks so much." I pushed them both toward the door. "Oh, and one last thing. Please keep the other passengers in the dark about this. No need to start a panic."

"In the dark," my mom said with a chuckle. "Good one."

I swear, even if she and Nan weren't related by blood, sometimes it was simply impossible to ignore the similarities they shared. Mom was far more pragmatic and a lot more normal than either Nan or me, but she belonged with us all the same.

We were a family, and nothing—not even newly exposed secrets—could change that.

CHAPTER TEN

After Dan and Melvin exited, I closed the door behind them and twisted the lock to ensure those of us who remained had some privacy.

"Mom, Dad, could you continue to search the room? I'm going to catch up with the cats," I said once I could no longer hear the departing men's footfalls in the corridor.

"Oh, sure, honey," Mom answered for them both. "We'll stay out of your way, Miss Pet Whisperer P.I." She was the one who had come up with that name for Octo-Cat's and my operation and was immensely proud of it —even though I secretly hated it. Talk about parading my secret for all to see! I pretended it was just a gimmick, but I had to wonder if the unusual name was the reason our firm hadn't received a single paying case to date.

"Let's go to the bed so we aren't in the way," I told the cats, but it was my dad who moved in the direction I had dictated.

I laughed awkwardly. He hadn't gotten used to this yet. Well, he was about to become very familiar with how things went when I was working a case with animal assistance.

"Oh, you meant…" He flashed his light toward Grizabella, and the startled feline hissed.

"Well, you have fun with that, then," he finished, backing slowly away.

"Why did you hiss at him?" I asked the Himalayan, not bothering to hide my irritation as I narrowed my eyes at her.

"He shone that bright light right in my eyes. It hurt!"

Ouch. Okay.

"Sorry, he didn't mean to." Again I wondered if I should pet her as a way of offering comfort, and again I decided against it. I had a sneaking suspicion that Grizabella didn't much like me, and I'd hate to actually be proven right while our investigation was still ongoing.

We settled on the bed. Given the way the comforter lay completely smooth, I guessed she hadn't tried going to sleep before meeting with her murderer. The cats each lay on a pillow, leaving me to sit farther down the mattress.

"Okay, what did you learn while you were out there?" I had no light with me but could make out their vague shapes in the spill-off from Mom and Dad's.

"Nothing," Grizabella answered for the both of them. She sounded almost bored.

"But you followed Dad the whole way, right?"

"We did," Octo-Cat assured me. "But we found nothing that drew our attention."

Well, I hadn't expected this. I was sure my kitty reconnaissance would turn off at least something helpful. "What about anyone who looked, sounded, or smelled familiar, Grizz?"

A threatening growl rose in the dark. "Don't call me Grizz. My name is Grizabella, and no, I didn't notice anything. Just as I told you before. This is hard for me, so please pay attention the first time around."

Yeesh, she sure made it hard to want to help her.

I took a deep breath and reminded myself that she was grieving and probably even more startled by Rhonda's murder than either me or Octo-Cat. We'd investigated deaths before, but Grizabella had never had to deal with anything like this.

Why would she? Why would anyone?

"I'm sorry," I said, hoping she'd believe the sincerity in my words. I truly did feel sorry for everything she'd gone through already, everything she'd still need to go through before this case was settled. "I just have a hard time believing this was a simple robbery. Someone wanted Rhonda dead, and I want to know why."

"Look at this!" Mom called from the bathroom, appearing in the doorway. From behind her, Dad shone his light on the object in her hands. An ornately carved wooden jewelry box.

"I don't think it was a robbery," she

mumbled, proving that we were on the exact same page. "Otherwise, why would they leave this behind? There's got to be thousands in diamonds and other precious stones in here."

Each necklace, bracelet, and pair or earrings she held up was more dazzling than the last. Many of the pieces boasted gigantic sapphires. And again I wondered if she chose the blue to match her cat's eyes.

"It's all silver," I pointed out. "But the necklace she wore when I met her in the dining car was gold and pearl."

Mom searched the ornate box, shaking her head. "Well, there's nothing like that in here."

Grizabella spoke from across the bed. "The necklace she wore today was her most prized possession. An important family heirloom handed down from her grandmother to her."

"So whoever took the necklace wanted the heirloom, but not the other, arguably even more valuable, pieces," I summed up for the humans who couldn't speak cat, rubbing my chin as I tried to make sense of all this.

"Or the killer struck for a completely different reason, saw an opportunity, and stole the necklace she was wearing but didn't think to search the room for other valuables," Mom ventured.

Dad nuzzled her from behind and kissed her neck. "I love seeing you in action. You're so smart."

"Not the time, guys," I spat, quickly looking away. Despite being an adult, I still hated seeing my mom and dad's flagrant and very public displays of affection.

"There is literally a dead body right there," I motioned toward Rhonda, hoping my parents turned their light to me in enough time to read the disapproving expression on my face.

"Sorry. We'll just keep searching," Dad said as Mom turned to take the jewelry box back into the bathroom.

"Grizabella," Octo-Cat said gently. "What can you tell us about your life with Rhonda? What kinds of things did you do? What kinds of places did you go?"

Good questions, especially since asking

Grizabella who would have wanted her owner dead would likely cause the Himalayan to either close right up or get overly emotional again.

The cat answered with a smile in her voice. "Rhonda was a very kind mistress. We traveled constantly, usually by train. Sometimes on a first-class jet. Mostly we went to cat shows, but sometimes we went places simply to take pictures of me amidst new scenery. I think Rhonda had a hard time staying put in one place because it reminded her of how lonely she'd let herself become."

Oh, this was good stuff. If Grizabella was willing to expand upon it, I was sure we'd learn something important.

"What do you mean?" I asked softly.

"I've been with Rhonda since I was a very small kitten. She's all I've ever known for my five human years in this world. Still, in all that time, she's never had visitors, never gone on dates, never done much of any of the things the humans do in television shows and movies."

"I love watching TV, too," Octo-Cat

butted in. "Do you like Law & Order? It's my favorite."

"Heavens, no," the other cat answered in disgust. "I much prefer love stories to those with blood and gore."

Octo-Cat stumbled over his response. "Oh, yeah. Right. Have you seen When Harry Met Sally? I really like the part when she—"

"Octavius," I interrupted, assuming he preferred his fancy name in the presence of our refined acquaintance. "This really isn't the time for that. We need to hear more about Rhonda. That's what's important now."

"Thank you," Grizabella said, surprising me with her politeness and the fact she'd acknowledged I'd done something right.

"Normally I love speaking about such frivolities, but normally my human is safe and sound beside me. Oh, my poor mistress..." Her words fell away, but then she shrieked the same terrible cry that first brought us to this car.

"And oh no! What will become of me, now that she's gone?"

I wished I had an answer for her, but unfortunately I knew even less than Grizabella did—especially if Rhonda had been as big a loner as she claimed.

CHAPTER ELEVEN

Grizabella yowled again.

"What's wrong?" Mom and Dad cried in unison.

"It's okay," I assured them. "Well, I mean, it's not exactly okay. She just realized she doesn't know where she'll go now that her owner's passed."

"Oh, poor sweet thing." Mom crossed the room along the edge and then petted the mourning Himalayan. "A nice, gorgeous girl like you will find a new home in no time."

Grizabella stopped shrieking but moved away from Mom's attempts to pet her. "I don't want a new home. I want my life with Mistress."

My heart broke for the newly orphaned feline. Since discovering Rhonda's body, we'd only worked toward solving her murder. None of us had taken any time to see how Grizabella was coping.

"Anyone could see how much Rhonda loved you. Heck, she even made a fan account for you on Instagram, and it has more than two-thousand followers."

"Yes, but those are fans," the cat responded with disdain. "I don't know a single one of them personally."

"Angela will figure something out," Octo-Cat promised, purring to show her it would all be okay. "She always does."

The doorknob rattled and then someone pounded against the door, bringing the tender exchange to an immediate halt.

"Hey," Dan yelled in his squeaky, pubescent voice. "Why is this thing locked?"

The frantic pounding started again, and Dad ran over to let him in. "Sorry about that!"

"We didn't want anyone stumbling in by accident," I explained, leaving out the part about taking the extra measure to protect my secret. "What's up? What did your bosses say?"

Dan looked back toward the door as if it had personally slighted him, then turned back toward us with lantern held high. "The police are on their way, but it could be a while given our remote location. Figures, right?"

"Yeah," I said amicably as my eyes struggled to adjust to the brightness of his lantern-style flashlight again. "Anything else? Do they know what stopped the train?"

He shook his head sadly and in obvious fear. "Only that it's been tampered with somehow. Whoever it was knew what he was doing, ensuring it would be next to impossible to get moving again without an expert mechanic familiar with this kind of train."

Crud.

Dan's expression lightened and he rocked his lantern playfully. "I do have good news, though."

Octo-Cat climbed onto my lap, and I drew strength from his calming presence. Seriously, this case was so different than usual.

We hadn't fought one bit. Perhaps we were evolving.

"Well, out with it already," Mom demanded. She only liked dramatic pauses when she was the one making them.

"The lights will be much easier to fix," Dan said, properly chastised. "Someone cut a few wires, but we've already found a passenger who says he knows how to fix it. He's working on it now."

"That is good news," Mom agreed, then flashed her phone at me. "And a lucky break for those who weren't responsible enough to charge up before the journey."

I groaned and pinched the bridge of my nose. A migraine wasn't exactly what I needed right now. "So at least our circumstances aren't getting worse," I reminded everyone.

"You girls stay in here," Dad instructed, moving toward the door. "Dan, bring that big light of yours and come with me."

I chased after him, refusing to be left behind. "Excuse me. None of that macho nonsense. Wherever you're going, I'm coming, too. So spill."

Dad sighed and placed his hand against the wall in defeat. "Why do you always have to assume it's something like that? I chose Dan because he has the best light and we're going to need it."

Yeah, there was no way I would be sitting out the next leg of our investigation. I turned to the young red-headed worker and held my hands out in supplication. "Dan, may I please borrow your light?"

He reluctantly handed it over, and I turned back to Dad with a giant smile of triumph. "You were saying?"

He chuckled at let out a low whistle. "You are just like your mother sometimes. C'mon, we're going to go nose around outside and see what we can find."

"Will you stay with my wife?" Dad asked Dan, and they shared a manly nod.

"I'm coming, too!" Octo-Cat called, jumping off the bed and joining us at the door.

"And I'm staying," Grizabella said, crossing her paws in front of her.

"Let's go, Dad," I said, lifting the lantern high as I followed him to the end of the car.

We found an exit toward the outside there, but it appeared to be jammed up tight. In the next car over, we found the door already slightly ajar, having swung back into the car a couple inches.

"Hopefully, somebody just needed a cigarette break really, really bad," Dad told me with a shrug and then pulled the door open the rest of the way so we could exit into the tunnel.

Very little space lay to either side of the train. Dad and I could walk side by side, but not comfortably. The stone walls pressed in close as we studied the gravel beside the tracks. Add in the intense darkness and it was almost like we'd been buried alive. Creepy.

Dad stopped walking and put out an arm to stop me, too. With his other hand, he pointed a few feet ahead. "Blood."

Sure enough, dark red droplets stained the light scattering of stones and pebbles. Even creepier.

"Did you see any earlier?" Dad asked, sweeping his phone light back toward the exit we used.

I shook my head soundlessly, then continued forward to see if the blood might form a trail.

"Stay by me," Dad called out, a quiver moving through his strong voice. "We don't know how close the murderer still is. For all we know, he could be right here hiding in the tunnel just a few feet away. And I'm not risking losing you."

I gulped and returned to his side.

Dad hooked his arm over my shoulders and pulled me close. "We do this together. Understand? You have my back, and I'll have yours."

"Awww. That's great for you guys. I'll go check things out on my own, though," Octo-Cat said, trotting off in the direction I'd just abandoned.

It worried me, him going off on his own, but what reason would a murderer have to hurt a random cat? There's no way the culprit could know that Octo-Cat was investigating this crime.

Dad and I moved slowly, using my light to illuminate our path and his to search the gravel. "I'm not seeing any more blood," he said. "Are you?"

I'd never been so disappointed not to find evidence of a violent crime. At least if we had a proper trail to follow, we'd know that the killer had left the train—and we may even be able to follow the drops to find him.

"No," I answered with a racking sigh. "Someone was definitely out here, and given how close the exit and the blood are to Rhonda's room, I'm guessing it was our killer. But I don't think he was injured. It's probably a bit of Rhonda's blood that dripped off his hands or something."

"But if he had the blood on his hands, wouldn't it be on the door?" Dad pointed out, continuing to move the tiny point of light from his phone around the path. "And also, why are we assuming the killer is a he?"

"Touché," I said. "It could definitely be a woman. Good thought, though. Let's go check out that door."

We closed the rest of the distance back to our entry and exit point, and I was just about to step through into the train when an anguished cry rang out from deeper in the tunnel.

A cat's cry.

"Octo-Cat!" I shouted and took off running. There was no way I was leaving him to face whatever danger lurked nearby on his own. I just hoped Dad could keep up.

CHAPTER TWELVE

"Angie, wait!" my dad yelled, but I kept running as fast as I could toward the spot where Octo-Cat had cried out into the black night. By the time I found him lying on his side amidst the gravel, I'd practically run out of breath both from the burst of exercise and my pumping adrenaline.

Please be okay. Please be okay.

Praying hard, I scooped him into my arms and clutched him against my chest. "What happened? Are you okay? Octo-Cat, talk to me!"

"Oof, take it down a couple notches, would you," he muttered, shaking his head as if my volume had physically injured him.

"What happened? Did you see the killer?" I demanded, searching his glowing amber eyes for answers.

"The killer? Of course not. I'd tell you if I found the killer." He actually had the audacity to laugh at me.

"Then why did you scream? I thought you were hurt."

Now that I knew my cat was okay, I wanted to wring his furry little neck for striking such fear straight into my poor pet-owning heart.

"I am hurt," he said with a low growl, then shifted in my arms and shoved a paw into my face. "I got a little rock or something stuck between my toe beans. See."

"That reaction was about your toe beans?" I practically screamed but then, remembering the need not to disturb the other passengers on the train, dropped my voice to a whisper yell.

"Don't act like you don't love them." He laughed again, and it took all I had to keep listening as he spoke. "Now can you please be a good human and dislodge this thing for me?"

Quickly, I plucked the pebble from his paw and tossed it away, then set him back on the ground.

"Thank you," he said, walking back toward our exit door with an exaggerated limp that I had no doubt he was faking for my benefit.

"What happened?" Dad asked, concern still etched in his features despite my utterance of the ridiculous phrase toe beans.

"Cat drama," I explained in a growl, still beyond angry at Octo-Cat for worrying me needlessly. "C'mon, let's go back to Mom and Dan."

We marched single file back toward the open door with me leading and Dad following. Once aboard, we stopped to inspect the door handle but found no blood marring its smooth surface. We did, however, find another spot on the carpet, only a few feet from the door, but—given the fact that each car was close to a hundred feet long—quite far from Rhonda's room.

Any dripping blood fell infrequently. No gushing here.

It was fully likely we'd find more if we

continued investigating outside the train, but the whole toe bean incident had spooked me thoroughly. It also made both Dad and I realize how vulnerable we were out there with no real way to protect ourselves.

"What did you find?" Mom asked, greeting us at the door to Rhonda's room and throwing her arms around Dad as if they'd been separated for days and not mere minutes. "I heard something, but Dan wouldn't let me go investigate."

"Good man," my dad said, giving the young redhead a fist bump.

"Nothing happened," I explained, then took on a cutesy voice I knew would drive my cat crazy. "The wittle kitty just got an ouchie in his wittle paw."

"Angela!" he cried, mouth gaping open in horror. "Not in front of another cat!"

Grizabella laughed, which made me laugh, too.

Dan just looked at me like I was certifiable. Maybe I was.

I returned his lantern to him, then caught everyone up on the droplets of blood Dad and I had discovered. "Did you find anything more in here?" I asked once I'd finished.

"Nope. You weren't actually gone all that long, you know," Dan answered, leaning back against the wall and crossing his arms.

Mom shrugged and offered me a weary smile. "Unfortunately, no."

We weren't going to solve anything by staying huddled together in this room. Someone had to search the train, and that someone was me.

"You guys keep searching here, and don't let anyone else inside," I said. "I'm going to see if I can find anything a bit further afield."

"Meaning you're going off by yourself," Dad summarized with a stern set to his jaw

"I'll take the cats," I said, drawing another strange look from Dan; he had the good grace not to say anything, though.

I didn't stick around to argue the point with my dad anymore. There were dozens, maybe hundreds of people aboard this train. And only one of them was a killer. That is, if the killer hadn't disembarked and run away like we now suspected.

I turned on my phone to guide our way.

Twelve percent battery left. Dan said the lights would be back on soon, and I was banking on that in a huge way now.

"Why are we doing a sweep of the passenger cars again?" Octo-Cat asked, obvious irritation laced in his nasally voice. Apparently, my little trick earlier had cost me his pleasant cooperation. This didn't bother me much, given that I was already well accustomed to working with a crabby tabby. Things actually felt more natural now.

"She doesn't trust us," Grizabella answered for me.

We moved into the next car, heading in the direction of the viewing car, dining car, and eventually our assigned seats. I paused after assuring no one had eyes on us.

"It's not that I don't trust you guys. I mean, of course I trust you guys. But sometimes things are worth a second look, right?"

"Uh-huh," Octo-Cat responded with a furious flick of his tail. "You're right. She doesn't trust us."

"Told you," Grizabella said, also flicking her fluffy tail. So glad they were bonding over this.

I sighed, then spoke while trying to keep the frustration from my voice. "Can you guys just... We're working together, not against each other. We all have the same goal here, so let's act like it."

That shut them up fast. Thank goodness for small miracles.

"Keep an eye out for any strange behavior, and keep trying to think of new ideas in case this doesn't work," I said when I was sure neither would hurl another argument at me.

"It won't work," Grizabella complained, and I had to bite my tongue to avoid flying into a full-scale lecture about what I'd only just said. Could she really not see how hard I was trying to help here?

Help for me came from an unlikely source. "She's trying her best," Octo-Cat explained softly. "Even if it's not very good."

Grizabella harrumphed but continued to follow me as I marched off toward the next car.

Oh, boy. I really hoped we'd find something on our tour of the train, because I'd love to make these cats eat crow.

CHAPTER THIRTEEN

Well, it looked like I'd be the one eating crow in the end.

Our sweep of the train turned up nothing, just as the cats had warned. Most of the passengers appeared to be sleeping. The few who had woken up seemed relaxed and unbothered, probably because they didn't know about the dead body that lay several cars back.

I corralled my feline companions into the tiny vestibule between cars to chat about what we should do next. "Before you say I told you so, listen up. We can't exactly shine lights in everyone's faces and ask them if they killed Rhonda."

"Why not?" Grizabella asked with a long, flat face as she sat back heavily on her haunches.

"Darling, please. Let the professionals talk." Octo-Cat raised a paw to the Himalayan's mouth to silence her. Wow, he had a lot to learn about women.

And, okay, perhaps I laughed a bit too hard when she bit him right on his poor injured toe bean. Served him right for condescending to her, especially after he saw what happened when I attempted to shorten her overly fancy name.

A whir sounded overhead, announcing the repaired electrical system. As the overhead lights popped backed on, muffled cheers rose from the cars on either side of us. People wanted to celebrate, but not wake their seatmates, which could definitely work to our advantage.

"Well, look at that." Octo-Cat deadpanned as I rubbed my eyes and wished for my sunglasses. "The lights are back on. Now, shall we return to plan A?"

"There wasn't a plan A," I reminded him

as bright spots danced at the edges of my vision.

"Then why was there a plan B?"

"Just listen!" I yelled. Enough was enough already.

Apparently, Octo-Cat was just as fed up with me as I with him. "Well, jeez. You don't have to yell," he rasped with his signature snark.

"Octavius, please," Grizabella interjected, scooting closer to him so that their furry bodies touched at the sides.

Thankfully—and probably just as Grizabella had suspected—this rendered the chatty tabby completely silent. Finally.

She nodded for me to continue with what I had to say.

"Most of the passengers are still asleep," I explained, keeping a close eye on Octo-Cat to make sure he wouldn't derail us yet again. "If the murderer is still on board, then he or she is definitely not just sleeping it off. That narrows our pool considerably. We couldn't find any suspicious behavior when we simply walked through the cars, so I think our next step should be to add a little pressure."

"Good plan. What did you have in mind?" Grizabella asked while Octo-Cat purred beside her.

"Nobody knows Rhonda's dead except the people we've spoken with… and, well, I guess the killer knows, too. I say we pretend to have an urgent message for her and use that as an excuse to talk to the passengers who are awake."

"But Mistress is dead. How can we have a message for her?"

"I know that, and we know that. But most of the people aboard don't know that, so asking them won't freak them out, right?"

Grizabella's eyes shone bright as understanding swept over her. "Oh, yes!"

"So we're just going to go up to each person we notice who's awake and ask if they know where we can find Rhonda?" Octo-Cat asked, rejoining the conversation with a sappy grin stretched between his whiskers. Ahh, the power of love.

"Pretty much," I said. "I'll do the talking, obviously. And you guys keep all your senses peeled."

Grizabella tilted her head to the side. "What does that—?"

"Human expression," my cat translated with a giant roll of his amber eyes.

"Sorry," I said with a chuckle. "You guys can smell changes in people's hormones, right? So if someone were to get really stressed by my questions, you could tell... Yes?"

"Yeah, humans are super easy to read," Octo-Cat responded haughtily. "Such simple creatures."

I scowled at him, then turned back to the Himalayan with a smile. Finally, she was on my side, and it felt great. "Are we ready to do this?"

"Let's." She rose to her feet and waited for me to open the door into the next car for her. We'd made our way back to the very front of the train a few cars in front of the one that held my family's seats.

"Excuse me," I said to a woman who sat with a sullen looking teenager who was immersed in her phone. Probably not our killer, but I had to talk to everyone to avoid suspicion. "Do you know where I can find

Rhonda Lou Ella Smith? I have an urgent message for her."

"Nope," she answered with a slight shake of her head. "I'm sorry. Good luck."

I'm going to need it.

I talked to several more people, both men and women of all ages, but not a single person showed any sign of recognizing the name. I checked with the cats between each car, just to make sure they hadn't found something.

They hadn't.

We entered the car that held our seats, and I immediately spotted a problem that I'd forgotten we had. Our special writer friend Melvin Mann paced up and down the aisle, talking to himself and eliciting the stares of every single person as he did. No one here was sleeping. Not a single soul.

"Melvin, what are you doing?" I shouted, rushing toward him.

"Trying to figure out the murder, of course," he told me, tapping a pen against the fingers on his other hand.

Someone cleared his throat across the aisle, and I laughed nervously. "Um, Mel.

This isn't the best time to plot out your next novel. These people are trying to sleep." I laughed again and shoved him toward the end of the car, hoping and praying that our culprit hadn't been sitting in that car while Melvin prattled on about all the pieces of evidence he'd either collected or overheard.

As we approached the vestibule, I rasped in his ear, "Go back to the car. Dan and my parents are there. They'll get you caught up." I was hoping they wouldn't tell our resident loose cannon anything, but I needed to offer something to get him to fall in line.

"What car?" he asked, twisting toward me. A garish smile split his face as he realized. "Oh, the scene of the murder."

I pushed him through the door. "Get out of here, and—for goodness' sake—try to keep a low profile."

"Hey, I'm a writer, not an actor." He lifted a hand overhead and shook his finger at no one in particular. Not an actor, but he sure was a character.

I stood in the vestibule, watching to make sure he kept going toward the sleeper cars without upsetting any more of the passengers.

Grizabella paced and flicked her tail impatiently. "What now?"

"We keep going and hope for the best." I thought back over the details of the night, then smiled. "He wasn't pacing and muttering to himself when we passed through the first time, so he must have just started when the lights turned back on. Just to be sure, I'll shoot my dad a text and ask him to collect Melvin and get him away from the rest of the passengers."

My fingers moved over the keyboard on my phone. Eight percent battery now, but we had light, which made the dying phone far less of a problem that it was before.

"Now, let's get on with our search," I told the cats, pushing into the next car, more determined than ever to find the murderer before circumstances beyond my control—or more specifically, Melvin—ruined everything.

CHAPTER FOURTEEN

I'd asked so many people if they knew where we could find Rhonda that my voice stung from overuse. The corners of my mouth also hurt from all the forced smiles. The cats and I had already hit up all the cars between the front of the train and the dining car, which meant there were only a few more to cross before arriving at the sleeper cars, and only a handful of those to try before we ran out of people to question altogether.

C'mon. C'mon, please. We have to find something.

I took a few more steps down the aisle, then turned to an older woman with shoulder-length black hair and large brown eyes rimmed with thick lashes. I could tell she'd been pretty in her youth because she was still stunning even now. She wore a hooded sweatshirt that you didn't often see women her age sporting, and she definitely didn't look like the type of person who'd have associated with Rhonda Lou Ella Smith, unless she was also a cat enthusiast.

I smiled and took a deep breath, leaning closer to her as I spoke. "Excuse me. Do you know where I can find Rhonda Lou Ella Smith?" I asked pleasantly, widening my smile as I waited.

She frowned and mouthed, "Sorry" without actually making a sound. Respecting her sleeping seatmate, how thoughtful. I'd been far less considerate in my search, jostling several passengers from sleep unintentionally.

"We've got a live one here!" Octo-Cat bellowed.

"She knows something," Grizabella confirmed in her melodic voice. "I can smell it all over her."

Showtime.

"Excuse me," I said to the woman who had already returned her attention to the paperback novel in her hands. "Are you sure you don't know Rhonda? It's really quite urgent."

"No. Now please let me return to my reading," she grumbled, then raised her book higher to block me out.

"She's lying!" Grizabella shouted. "She's lying!"

I pushed the book down and forced the woman to look me in the eye. "I'm sorry, but if you don't know Rhonda, then why are you acting so nervous?"

"Nervous?" she asked, then laughed nervously. How convincing. "I'm not nerv—"

"No more lies!" Grizabella cried, jumping right onto the woman's lap and unleashing a terrible hiss.

"G-G-Grizabella?" the woman stuttered. "What are you—?"

"So you do know her!" I widened my stance to block her into her seat in case she tried to make a run for it. I might be angering a violent criminal, but at least the train car was filled to the brim with witnesses. She wouldn't be so bold as to try anything in front of them… Would she?

The woman set her book down without even bothering to adjust the bookmark. "What's the message? Perhaps I can give it to her."

"It's really quite urgent. Would you come with me? The conductor's been searching for anyone connected with Rhonda, because we need your help. Urgently." Ugh. I needed to keep repeating urgent over and over again like it was some kind of magic passcode.

"But I thought you said you had a message for her?"

"Yes, and for you. Now will you join me, or should I call security?" I didn't even know if this train had security, but the threat worked to get the woman out of her seat.

I surreptitiously texted my mom and asked her to meet me in the viewing car so we could escort the woman back to Rhonda's room together. For all I knew, she was the killer and could try to take me out at the first opportunity.

As much as I trusted my cat partners to want to protect me, they were no match for a human with a weapon and a motive. I needed to keep her talking as I walked behind her and guided her toward the sleeper cars. Maybe she hadn't figured out that I suspected her—or at least not yet.

"I'm Angie," I explained. "The conductor asked me to keep an eye on Grizabella since I have a cat of my own with me on the train," I yammered on. I needed to stop going on about the conductor every few minutes, but I didn't know what the other train people were called and I wanted to sound official.

"Is Rhonda okay?" the woman asked, trying to look back at me over her shoulder as we continued to stumble forward.

"Oh, yes," I lied, needing to get her somewhere private—and with backup—before sharing the truth. "Thank goodness we found you just in time. Say, how do you know her?"

"Oh, um, well, she's my sister. Half-sister, actually," she corrected herself immediately, then added, "We weren't close."

"I know how that goes," I said with a smile in case she looked back again. I was an only child, but I would do anything I could to keep her talking and moving, anything to build up some kind of rapport, seeing as it could just save my life. "What's your name?"

"Sariah Smith," she mumbled. "Will this take long?"

"Almost there," I promised as we finally headed into the viewing car. My mom was already there waiting.

"I know you," Sariah said, stopping in her tracks and raising a hand to point at my mother. "You're—"

Mom's hand shot out in greeting. "Laura Lee, Channel Seven News, serving Blueberry Bay, the great state of Maine, and now the full Northeastern Seaboard."

"I watch you on the news," Sariah stuttered. "What are you doing here? Investigating a story?" She glanced back toward the rear exit, but Mom placed a firm hand on her shoulder.

I moved toward the other end of the car, but Sariah didn't follow.

Mom jumped in to help out. "Yes, I'm investigating a story. And I need to speak with you, if you'll just come with me."

"Um, don't I need to sign a waiver or something?"

"Nope. This one's off the record.

C'mon." Mom shoved her perhaps a bit too forcibly into the next car.

"Almost there," I assured her again, practically pulling her as Mom pushed from behind now.

"I don't think I can—" Sariah grunted. I'd have felt bad had I suspected she was innocent in all of this, but as the cats had said, she reeked of guilt. Even I could practically smell it with my weak human olfactory sense.

"And we're here," Mom announced before Dad swung open the door to Rhonda's room.

Sariah screamed the moment her eyes fell on Rhonda's dead body. She tried to run, but Mom and I formed a barrier in the doorway, blocking her misguided attempt at escape.

Sariah sobbed, choked, and screamed again. "Oh my gosh, what happened to Rhonda? Help, help, help! Somebody get me out of here!"

"We need to shut her up," Dad cried as Sariah continued to shout and shove at me and Mom. "What should we do?"

Melvin darted forward, a weapon held at

waist height but disguised by his jacket. All I could see was an ominous bulge along with the manic rage splashed across his face, but from the way he postured, I was sure it had to be a gun under there. "Quiet, or I'll give you a reason to be quiet."

Oh my gosh, this was wrong on so many levels. A very big part of me wanted to tie Melvin up and stash him somewhere so he couldn't cause any more problems.

But then Sariah stopped crying and started confessing everything.

CHAPTER FIFTEEN

"Everyone calm down," Dad said in a patient, measured voice that must have been so hard to keep, given the current circumstances. He bravely stepped forward and inserted himself between Melvin and Sariah, daring either of them to continue acting out. "There's no need for things to turn violent."

Melvin stepped around dad and narrowed his gaze on Sariah. "There is, if she doesn't start talking and fast."

"That's not ne—"

"He wasn't supposed to hurt her!" Fat tears rolled down Sariah's cheeks and onto her sweatshirt. "You have to believe me. I didn't know he was going to hurt her."

"Who?" I asked from the doorway, anxiety ripping the words from my throat. If Melvin shot at Sariah, the bullet would likely tear into me, too. I so did not feel like dying today.

"Who wasn't supposed to hurt her?" I asked again when she failed to answer.

Our witness cried so hard she staggered forward, barely able to keep herself on her feet.

Mom draped Sariah's arm over her shoulder and guided her over to the bed. "C'mon, sweetie. It's okay. You're safe with us."

Melvin followed, his weapon still threatening from beneath his jacket. "That's right. As long as you keep talking, then you have nothing to worry about." I wanted to bonk him on the head. Couldn't he see that he was terrifying everyone around him?

Dan twisted the lock on the door, then looked to my father for guidance, who crossed his arms over his chest and took up sentinel at the room's one exit point.

It was like we were billiard balls. All of us suddenly rearranging, bouncing into new positions, staying near the edges of the room. I moved close to where Rhonda still lay splayed across the floor. That way, every time Sariah spoke to me, she'd be forced to glance upon her dead half-sister. It wasn't to be cruel, but rather to keep her honest and remind her how much was at stake here.

Not just for her, either. For all of us.

"Who wasn't supposed to hurt her?" I pressed again, keeping my voice kind and hopefully free of judgment.

Sariah sniffled and shook her head. Perhaps we needed a more indirect approach to ease her into talking.

"You know, I met her," I said with a far-off smile, even though the past I was remembering had only happened several hours prior. "We sat together for a while in the dining car and talked cats."

Mom handed Sariah a tissue from her purse, and she blew her nose into it. "That sounds like Rhonda all right."

"I thought you weren't close," I pointed out, again trying my best not to sound accusing even though Sariah had for sure played some part in the crimes that had happened aboard this train tonight.

She shook her head and balled the tissue in her first. "We weren't, but I follow her online. That's how I recognized Grizabella."

The cats. I hadn't noticed where they'd gone.

"Over here," my tabby called from near the bathroom, either reading my mind or sensing the worry that crept up on me when I realized I'd lost sight of him.

I turned toward him and smiled upon spotting him unharmed and unafraid.

Grizabella, however, stared at Sariah with fierce, unblinking eyes. She needed the answers, needed to know why this horrible thing had happened to her mistress.

"You said he wasn't supposed to hurt her," I reminded Sariah again, approaching my follow-up differently this time. "What was he supposed to do instead?"

Sariah shook her head and peered at me through red-rimmed eyes. Apparently, my sudden change in questioning had thrown her. "He was only supposed to take what's ours. That's it."

"And what was that?"

"The necklace."

The image of that beautiful piece of jewelry flashed in my mind's eye. Pearls, gold, amazing craftsmanship, but worth killing for? Not to me.

"The family heirloom?" I asked.

"Yes, she was wearing it tonight. I saw her when she came off the train to speak with us at the Bangor station."

That's right. I knew I'd seen her on the platform. With Sariah here, all the pieces were finally starting to feel like they belonged to the same puzzle. Soon we may even be able to discern the picture. I suspected I knew what happened next but asked anyway. "What did you talk about?"

"We asked for the necklace back. She never should have gotten it." Sariah balled both of her hands into fists, then let them go, looking at me with equal parts anger and sorrow.

"I'm guessing she said no."

"He barely even got two words out before she turned away and ran back for the train."

"Then what happened?" I asked.

All the others in the room remained quiet as Sariah and I continued our conversation. They all needed to hear this, too.

She turned to Mom and addressed her answer there. "He said that one way or another the necklace would be ours, and then we followed her onto the train. He knew she would say no, so we were already ready with the tickets."

"And what was the next part of your plan? What were you supposed to do after she said no?"

"Not my plan. His. I was supposed to find a way to stop the train in the middle of the night so that he could pay her a visit and take the necklace back. Then we were going to meet in the viewing car and exit together from there."

"But you're still here," I pointed out with raised eyebrows.

Sariah faced me once more. "Yes. He never showed up."

Desperation clawed at the edges of my

brain. I so badly wanted to know who the he in Sariah's story was, but there were other details I needed to find out first—rather than risk her breaking down again.

"Why did you both want the necklace so badly?"

"It rightfully belonged to us. It had been passed down for generations, long before our ancestors ever settled in America. Not only is it worth a fortune, it has sentimental value, too."

"So it's a family thing, but you said yourself that Rhonda was family." I crossed my arms over my chest and waited, hoping my words had the incendiary effect I wanted. If so, they could blow this whole thing open and finally get Sariah to reveal the identity of her mysterious partner, the he.

"No." She closed her eyes and her cheeks turned red, but still she spoke. "Her family took everything from us. And it was a cold, hard slap to the face when Father gave the necklace to her instead of one of us."

I didn't say anything, hoping Sariah would volunteer more on her own. When she didn't, someone else stepped in.

"How did her family hurt yours, sweetie?" Mom asked from her spot beside the sobbing witness. Most of her tears had dried up now, however, anger taking their place.

"When I was five, my father left to start a new family. He said he had fallen in love and the lady was pregnant, so he had no choice. But he did have a choice! He just didn't choose us. He left and he took everything from us. All of the money and privilege that should have been our birthright went to the new family, went to Rhonda. So, when he told me his plan to get our necklace back, of course, I wanted to help. Wouldn't you?"

"I understand where you're coming from," I said, nodding along. "I also believe that even though you hated Rhonda, you hadn't planned for her to die."

She straightened and sat taller on the bed. Some of the tension drained from her fists and tightly set jaw.

There, I'd given her something important. Now she had to help by providing that final piece we so desperately needed. "Can you do me one last favor and tell me whose plan it was? We need to know who hurt Rhonda so that we can make sure you and everyone else on this train stays safe."

"He's not going to lay a finger on me. I'll kill him first," Sariah said between clenched teeth, and I believed her.

"But who is he? Who's he, Sariah?" I practically begged now.

"He is our brother. Jamison."

CHAPTER SIXTEEN

All eyes were on Sariah, including mine.

"There," she growled at Melvin, who still held his weapon at the ready. "I've told you everything I know, so how about you stop threatening me with that gun or knife or whatever you have in there?"

Melvin snickered and pulled the weapon from his jacket, causing us all to flinch as he tossed it onto the bed beside Sariah. "As they say, the pen is mightier than the sword." The smug grin on his face showed just how clever he felt he'd been.

Sure enough, a gold-tipped fountain pen lay on the comforter, shining in the light cast down from overhead. A pen!

Crazy Melvin had proven useful, after all.

"Gotcha!" he cried, and I half-expected him to break out into an endzone-style victory dance.

A collective groan rose throughout the room.

Sariah sneered at the false weapon, then picked it up and threw it back toward Melvin. "Figures."

"How did you stop the train?" Dad asked, pointedly ignoring Melvin.

The writer withered when he realized we wouldn't spend the rest of the night applauding his clever ruse. But our investigation was far from over. We still hadn't caught the killer.

"That's easy for a mechanical engineer," Sariah answered with a casual shrug.

"No one has been able to get the engine going again, but they were able to get power back," Dan added from his place beside Dad.

Our witness chuckled wearily. "Lights, that's electrical engineering. Not my area."

Clearly, this woman was very educated. Being abandoned by a parent definitely sucked, but did she really end up having such a bad life? Were things truly bad enough for Jamison to murder Rhonda as a way of paying for their father's sins? Everything in me screamed no.

My own family had a twisted backstory, one Mom and I had only recently discovered and still didn't quite understand. But I would never in a million years hurt someone for answers—or for revenge.

I guess that's why I was the P.I. and not the murderer. And thank goodness for that!

"Have you seen Jamison since the train stopped?" I asked, remembering my role.

"No. Like I said, he never turned up at our meeting spot. The jerk probably made a run for it without me."

"He was probably trying to frame you for it," Melvin pointed out. "That's what I would do if I had to write a character like that. As a novelist, I mean."

When still no one gave him the attention he craved, Melvin cleared his throat, then quieted again.

"We did find a bit of blood outside the train," Dad offered, bringing all eyes to him.

Sariah sighed and fell back on the bed, making us all tense. "Well, then, there you go. Betrayed by both my siblings in one night. Yay me."

"Sariah," Mom said gently. "I don't think Rhonda ever meant to hurt you. It's not her fault, what happened with your family. Things were probably hard for her growing up, too."

"She was lonely all the time," Grizabella said softly from her spot by the bathroom. "My poor, poor mistress."

Since Sariah couldn't understand Grizabella's words, she spoke over them. "Well, whatever the case, I'm sure the cops are on their way to arrest me, and meanwhile Jamison gets away with the whole thing."

"He's not going to get away with it," I promised. "We know it was him, and I'm sure the police will agree." We'd solved the murder. Catching the bad guy should be the easy part, right?

Sariah sat up and shook her head bitterly. "Yeah, but he's gone. He got away."

"Not necessarily," Octo-Cat piped up as

he crossed the room to stand at my side. "Remember how cats are superior to humans in pretty much every way?"

I wanted to respond to that—if only to set the record straight, lest he later claim I had agreed with him—but we had a room full of people who didn't know my secret. Instead of asking him to explain himself, I widened my eyes at him, willing him to explain.

Thankfully, he understood. "Yeah, yeah, you don't want to talk in front of the others. Anyway, cats are awesome. Cats are the best, and this cat can find that killer who's on the loose."

"Yes!" Grizabella cried in delight. "Yes, we can sniff him out. Brilliant idea, my darling."

Octo-Cat became stock still, turning only at his neck to stare at the Himalayan with bright, beseeching eyes. "Your darling?"

She nuzzled him and purred. Everything about her softened. "And my hero."

Octo-Cat melted like a giant slab of butter. "Oh, Grizabella. I'm so glad you love me back! I will devote all my lives to you. At least all the ones I have left. I will never let you down. I—"

"Will you help avenge my mistress?" Grizabella asked pointedly.

"Oh, yeah, baby."

The cat soap opera playing out before me would have been cute under any other circumstances, but right now, we had a bad guy to catch.

"Sariah, I have an idea," I said, eager to get on with it.

"Sure, it was your idea," Octo-Cat scoffed, then immediately went back to cuddling and licking his new girlfriend.

"What I told you before about watching Grizabella because I have a cat, too, that was true. But I didn't tell you that my cat is also a highly trained stunt cat. We were, uh, on our way down to Georgia to do some work on an upcoming film before all this happened. Anyway, Octavius here is extremely well trained, and I think if we give him something of Jamison's, he could use it to track the scent and find our guy."

Sariah studied Octo-Cat as if trying to

decide whether he was up to the task. In the end she frowned and said, "Great thought, but Jamison's probably made it pretty far by now. What's the point?"

"Probably. But, then again, do you know how fast a cat can run?"

"I'm not really familiar with—"

"Up to thirty miles per hour," Melvin interjected, waving his phone to show us he'd found the answer in record time.

Sariah quirked an eyebrow and glanced at Octo-Cat again. "Okay, that's pretty fast, but how are you sure your cat will even stay on his trail? And aren't you a little worried about sending him out there on his own? It sounds like he's really valuable if he's a celebrity and all that."

"Well…" I pretended to hesitate, seeing as Sariah seemed to need a few more moments to get on board with the idea. "Let's just say I trust him, and I know he can do this for us."

"I've seen him in action before," Mom said from her perch on the bed. "And she's right, that cat is pretty incredible."

"Thank you, thank you," Octo-Cat said, waving his paw at his subjects.

Grizabella cooed and cuddled closer to his side.

Dad asked what we all needed to know. “So do you have something of Jamison’s or not?”

CHAPTER SEVENTEEN

Sariah took off the hooded sweatshirt she wore, revealing a beautiful fitted blouse beneath. "This is his," she said, tossing the sweatshirt to me, then reaching her arms up to hug herself and replace the lost warmth.

"Thanks. I'll get him started on the scent outside. Everyone else stay here. He doesn't work as well with a crowd."

"Why not?" Grizabella asked, intertwining her tail with Octo-Cat's in what had to be the feline version of footsie. "I love an adoring audience."

He lifted his head and sniffed the air for no obvious reason. "She says things like that sometimes so the other humans don't figure out she can talk to us."

"Octavius!" I called, moving toward the door and making a clicking noise. "Here kitty!"

He groaned as he trotted after me. "Enough with the kitty already. You know I don't like that."

Grizabella followed us outside into the dark tunnel. Luckily, the now illuminated train cars cast enough light to save me from having to use my remaining battery on the flashlight function.

I set Jamison's sweatshirt on the ground. "Can you get anything from this?" I asked my cat.

He took a big whiff of the fabric, then sneezed. "Whoo, boy. It's got that lady's stench all over it. There is a thing as too much perfume, honey."

"A lady can never make too many efforts with her presentation," Grizabella purred. Leave it to a D-list Instagram celebrity to side with vanity.

I bit my lip and said a silent prayer for patience. The thing about working with cats was that it would always be on their timetable.

"Can you smell him, too? Or is she too overpowering?" If this didn't work, I had no idea what else we could do, especially since Sariah seemed to believe that her brother would have no trouble evading the authorities.

"Yeah, I got him, too." Octo-Cat yawned and stretched each of his four legs, one by one—showing off for his lady friend, no doubt. "Let's do this!"

She appeared to swoon at his heroic catliness. Whoo, boy, indeed.

"Wait." I crouched down, so that I was closer to his height. "I don't have a way to track you. We didn't bring your pet GPS and my phone is going to die any minute. It's dangerous, and you're going it alone. Can you promise me—?"

"He's not going alone." Grizabella stood, fierce determination swirling in her blue eyes. "I'm going, too."

"My love, I couldn't possibly ask this of you. As Angela said, it's dangerous. I've already injured one toe bean in pursuit of this investigation. I could never risk your lovely toe beans like that." Octo-Cat nuzzled Grizabella, but she stepped away before he could make contact.

"Rhonda was my human. I owe this to her." The Himalayan took a deep breath and then took off in an impossibly fast run. The only time I'd ever seen Octo-Cat move anywhere near that fast was on the rare occasion when he had the zoomies—and we weren't allowed to talk about that.

"What a woman!" he said, taking one glance back at me before sprinting after her.

"But I don't know how I'll find you!" I called into the lonely tunnel, but it was too late. Both cats had already disappeared from view.

Please, please, be safe.

I turned back toward the train and found Dad waiting in the doorway.

"I wanted to give you some privacy in case you needed it," he said, stepping down to join me on the gravel. "Is everything okay?"

I looked back down the tunnel longingly. "Yeah. I just worry about the dangerous things he gets himself into sometimes."

Dad laughed. "Believe me, I know how that goes. Both you and your mom are going to put me in an early grave."

I shivered, not wanting to think about my dad or anyone else dying. I'd already seen more than enough to last a lifetime. Some occupational hazards were harder to accept than others.

"We'll do anything to take care of our kids. That's what being a parent is about." Dad's voice was soft, kind. "And before you say anything, yes. A pet parent is still a parent."

Octo-Cat would hate hearing himself referred to as my child, but sometimes it really felt as if he were. I knew Mom and Nan would move mountains to protect me, too. I'd always been loved, protected, valued…

And suddenly I knew that Dad's words referred to so much more than their surface meaning. "Nan and my real grandparents," I stated simply.

Dad nodded. "Just because you're not blood, that doesn't mean she isn't your real family," he said, echoing my thoughts from earlier. "She gave up so much to keep your mom safe, even though she didn't know why at the time."

"We still don't know why." I wanted to know so badly for myself, for my mom, but more than anything, for Nan who had lived her whole life having no idea why this strange, scary, and even wonderful thing had happened to her.

Dad chuckled again. "Between you and your mom? You'll figure it out in no time. If there's one thing I've learned in life, it's to always bet on my girls."

I wrapped my arms tight around him. Even though we'd never been very close, I'd never had to doubt his love for me.

"This whole trip has been a lot," I told him once we released our embrace. "I just don't know if I have the energy for two weeks meeting the family now."

"Then we'll go home. Just as soon as we can get off this danged train, anyway." He glanced around, then chuckled again. The tension lessened with each sound of my dad's laugh. It was one of my safe places. "Well, you know what I mean. As soon as we're out of this tunnel and allowed to officially disembark."

"Won't they be mad, though? The family in Georgia?" As much as this entire situation wrung my heart out like a soapy dishrag, I was still excited to meet them, to see our family grow despite the unusual circumstances. Could I really risk ruining that?

Dad shook his head and smiled reassuringly. "We've waited this long to meet them. Heck, we didn't even know they existed until a few weeks ago. It can wait—they can wait—until you're rested and ready."

"That's good. Because I really need to get home and be with Nan," I said, desperate to be reunited with my favorite person. Nan had raised me. She'd become my very best friend, and I just didn't feel normal without knowing she was nearby.

"I know you do," Dad said, and we hugged again. "I know you do."

CHAPTER EIGHTEEN

Just over half an hour later, the police arrived and swept through the train. They kicked us out of Rhonda's room to secure the scene. While two officers investigated the body, another officer took Mom, Dad, me, Sariah, Dan, and Melvin to the viewing car to keep an eye on us while a detective questioned us one by one outside.

"I hadn't met Rhonda before the train, no," I assured the detective, but I could sense the suspicion lingering in her eyes.

She looked down and referenced her notebook. I had to wonder how well she could actually see in the dim light of the tunnel.

"Then why did you spend nearly two hours with her in the dining car?" she asked.

And I answered with a shrug. "Just being friendly."

"Angela! Angela!" Octo-Cat bellowed in the distance.

"Did you hear that?" the detective asked me, tilting her head to listen.

"Angela! Angela!" he cried again. To the detective, his words probably sounded like a horrible caterwauling.

"Yes, I think it's my cat," I said, equally excited and afraid of what news he would bring.

"Strange noise for a cat to make," the detective observed.

"Angela! Angela!" my cat cried again, growing closer and closer to where we stood. A few moments later his fuzzy body hurtled into mine, and he screamed again. "Angela! Angela!"

"Stand back, that animal could be dangerous!"

"He's just my cat. See." I scooped Octo-Cat up and cuddled him to my chest to show her he meant no harm.

He panted heavily, which he never did. The poor guy must have been running for a very long time—or be very, very stressed. I was hoping for the former.

"Can we get him some water?" I asked her as his panting continued unchecked.

"No... time," he wheezed, then hacked, then tried to speak again. "Griz... abella. We... have to... go to her!"

The detective studied me carefully. "Ma'am, is everything okay?"

Ma'am? I was younger than she was. Okay, not important right now. I needed to figure out my next step, and I needed to do it in a way that didn't raise suspicion.

Earlier that night I'd told Dan, Sariah, and Melvin that I was a celebrity pet trainer as an excuse for setting Octo-Cat on the trail. And now it was time to take on another false persona with the detective. I just hoped she would buy it.

I swallowed hard and then raised my eyes to meet her questioning gaze head on. "I know this may seem a bit unorthodox, but I'm a psychic, you see, and I believe the victim's ghost is telling me where to find her killer."

She placed a hand on her hip. "Her ghost?"

"Yes." Sorry, Rhonda, but this is the best way to catch him. "Rhonda says he's moved quite a way from the train. We'll need a vehicle to get to him."

"Yes, good!" Octo-Cat cheered. His words seemed to be coming more easily now. "I can take you… to her. To them."

The detective tipped her chin and quirked an eyebrow. "So you need a police escort?" she asked slowly, either to mock me or to make sure she understood.

"I know it's crazy, but—"

"Let's go," the detective said, surprising me with her sudden agreeableness. "Our department has been known to work with psychics from time to time, and right now you're the best lead we've got. The cruiser's about half a mile that way." She pointed down the tunnel, then turned back to me. "Try anything funny, though, and I won't hesitate to make an arrest."

When I nodded my consent, she took off in the direction she'd pointed earlier. It was the opposite way from the path Octo-Cat had taken to return to us.

I followed, keeping Octo-Cat in my arms because I could tell he needed the rest. While I grew more tired, he regained some of his strength.

"We found him," he explained as my feet scrambled for purchase on the uneven terrain. "And Grizabella was marvelous. She scratched him up real good. He threw her, and I think she may have gotten hurt. But she wouldn't leave his side. She sent me back to get help while she continued to track the bad guy."

Well how about that? Grizabella had proven to be the hero, after all.

I just hoped she was okay from the injury she sustained during her fight with Jamison. I hated not being able to comfort Octo-Cat while we were in the presence of the detective, but I had to believe he understood that I would do everything I could for both Grizabella and Rhonda.

At last we reached the end of the tunnel and broke out into the open sky. The sun had just begun to rise, infusing the clouds with celestial fire—beautiful and eerie at the same time. The cruiser sat facing the tunnel, and the detective and I both bolted for it.

I climbed in the back, just in case I was still a suspect. We'd already lost so much time, and I couldn't cost us anymore until I knew that Grizabella was safe, and Jamison had been apprehended.

"You can sit up front, you know," the detective said, studying me in the rear-view mirror. A smile crept across her face as she spoke. So maybe I wasn't a suspect, after all.

"I can't smell anything from in here," Octo-Cat informed me from the footwell. Either the detective hadn't noticed I'd brought him along or didn't really mind.

"I'm fine back here," I assured her, buckling in for what was sure to be a wild ride. "But could you please roll down the windows? My, uh, powers work better when I'm one with nature."

She nodded and lowered both of the front windows.

"Ahh, that's better. They're this way." Octo-Cat moved his body to the car's left.

"Let's start by going left," I told the detective.

The engine roared to life, and we were off.

"How fast should I be going?" she asked, and I had no idea what to tell her.

Octo-Cat moved to the right of the footwell. "This way, but not too much this way."

"Make a right, but not a full right," I instructed, ignoring her earlier question, focusing on what I did know instead of what I didn't.

She guided the cruiser in the direction I'd indicated.

"Too far. Too far!" Octo-Cat cried and moved back toward the left.

"Um, less right than that," I said. "Bring it back to the center a little."

Man, it was hard to give driving directions when there were no roads and I had no idea where we were actually going. Still, I trusted my cat, and I knew he'd get us there one way or another.

"Perfect," he said after the detective had finished her course correction. He hopped onto the bench seat beside me and then climbed onto my lap. "Now straight on to my Grizabella."

CHAPTER NINETEEN

We drove for a good twenty minutes before I finally spotted movement on the horizon.

Octo-Cat noticed her at the exact same time as me. He screeched and dug his claws into my lap. "She's there! My beautiful Grizabella! We've found her!"

Sure enough, the Himalayan trotted across the landscape ahead. Her beautiful fur appeared almost ghastly in the soft morning light and her once perfect gait now fell unevenly, but she was alive and still moving forward. I had to admire her determination to see this through.

Even though she'd seemed more than a bit spoiled when I first met her, she was a good cat. A really good cat.

"Suspect sighted." The detective jolted her cruiser forward even faster than before, then veered to a stop.

"Tell Rhonda's ghost she did a good job," she told me before racing outside to chase the man hobbling down the hill.

Octo-Cat sprinted through the open door after her, but rather than following the detective, he turned back the way we'd come. "My darling! My darling!" he cried.

As much as I wanted to help, I stayed put in the back of that cop car and sent a quick text to my parents in a group chat: We found Jamison. Detective is apprehending him right now. All is good.

And with that, my battery finally gave out, rendering my phone useless.

Less than five minutes later, the detective returned, dragging a handcuffed man along with her. "Get to the front, psychic," she barked at me.

As soon as I got out, she shoved Jamison in. For a moment, my eyes met his and I was surprised to see that they weren't cold or calculating. Instead, they appeared soft, kind, not so unlike my father's. A smattering of freckles on his cheeks and nose gave him a boyish appearance. Bloody scratches covered his arms, and his shirt had even been slashed through, thanks, no doubt, to Grizabella's attack.

This guy didn't look like a killer at all, and yet I had no doubt he'd done the deed.

"Meet me outside the tunnel," the detective murmured into her radio as she brought the police cruiser back to life.

"Wait!" I shouted, panic rising in my chest. "My cat!"

"I'm bringing the witness back, then taking the suspect in," the detective continued on, ignoring me completely.

The cruiser hadn't picked up much speed yet, so I swung open the door, unbuckled my seatbelt, and prepared to jump. Seeing what I was up to, she hit the brakes hard, jerking me clear out of the car.

I fell to the cold ground, landing on my back in such a way that all the air whooshed out of my lungs. Ouch.

Despite the nagging pain, there was no time to waste. I was okay, and I had to make sure the cats were, too. I sat up in a hurry, wincing from the pain of making such a sudden movement.

"Oh, Angela," Octo-Cat said with a light-hearted chuckle as he and Grizabella approached from nearby. Despite her limp and obvious fatigue, they fell into perfect step beside each other. "I may be a stunt cat, but you are definitely not a stunt human."

I couldn't tell whether he was just giving me a hard time or if he actually believed the lie I'd said about him earlier. Knowing him, I'm sure he believed every word of it.

"You were very brave," the Himalayan told me with an approving nod.

"But not as brave as you, darling," Octo-Cat cooed in that special lovestruck voice he reserved expressly for his new girlfriend. "You were marvelous. Miraculous, even."

She giggled, and I pushed myself back to my feet with more difficulty than I would have liked. Ouchie ouch ouch. "C'mon, guys. Let's get back to our ride."

I let myself back in through the passenger side and both cats leaped up to join me.

The detective did not look happy. "That stays between us," she said in a low growl. "I'm already going to get a hard time for consulting a psychic on this case. The last thing I need is for the guys at the station to hear about you hurling yourself from the car before we even hit ten miles per hour."

"But you said—"

"I know what I said. Turns out you're not the only one who can bend the truth a little to get the job done." She glanced at Octo-Cat, then back toward me and winked.

My jaw hit my chest. Not really, but whoa. What? How could she possibly…?

No, it didn't matter. Even though I had no idea how she'd figured it out, I knew my secret would be safe with the detective.

By the time we made it back to the tunnel —and thus the train—the sun hung high in the sky and the day was alive with energy. The detective's partner waited with Mom and Dad outside the tunnel.

When they saw me get out of the cop car,

they ran forward. Mom hugged me from the left, and Dad hugged me from the right.

"Why are you all dirty?" Mom swatted at my pants, trying to brush the mud and dirt away. I glanced down and saw just how messy I'd gotten as a result of my fall from the cruiser.

Oh, well. Clothes could be cleaned or, if needed, replaced. What we'd all just been through together was worth so much more.

"It's a long story," I hedged. "What time is it, anyway?" I asked, suddenly feeling the weight of fatigue washing over me. I'd only gotten a few hours of sleep sitting in the viewing car before this latest murder mystery had consumed the rest of the night and early morning hours.

"Why don't you check your phone?" Dad asked with a smirk.

"I can't because it—" I stopped and laughed sarcastically when I realized his joke. My parents were never going to let me live my low phone battery down.

"It's about seven thirty," Mom said, stifling a yawn of her own. "Dad told me you were thinking about heading home instead of finishing our trip down to Larkhaven."

Guilt washed over me. Mom had really been looking forward to this trip, and now I'd ruined it for her. No, this was important. I could summon strength and mental fortitude from somewhere. "Yeah, but we don't have to if—"

Mom shook her head and smiled. "I think it's a great idea. I'll call the family in a couple of hours and let them know. Hopefully, by then the techs will have us moving again. We heard they were bringing in a new engine to take us back to the nearest station."

I met my mom's smile with one of my own. "Smart. Even if they continue, I bet nobody's going to want to keep traveling aboard that murder train. At least I wouldn't want to."

We stood together, watching the police work, saving up our energy for the half-mile walk back through the tunnel. I watched as Octo-Cat tended to his girlfriend's wounds in a nearby patch of grass.

Sure, their love story was still on its first chapter, but already he was a changed cat.

My heart ached, knowing that we may never get the chance to see her again, to even know where she'd ended up.

"You're worried about her. Aren't you?" Dad asked, motioning toward the Himalayan with his chin.

"She loved Rhonda, and now she has no idea what's going to happen to her next." An idea struck me, allowing a brief burst of hope to fill me up. "Do you think Sariah will take her?"

"I think Sariah will go to prison as an accessory to murder," Mom said with a sigh. "Or at least for tampering with the train. Such a shame."

"Then what about Grizabella?" I asked, trying not to cry before we knew for sure what would happen. She'd literally lost everything when Rhonda died, and like Octo-Cat, she was accustomed to having only the best things in life. Would a new owner know how to care for her properly?

"I don't know, sweetie," Mom said, kissing the side of my head. "We can only hope for the best."

She was right. Grizabella's fate was out of

our hands for now, but I would definitely be following up with the police every single day until they could tell me what had happened to her.

I owed it to Octo-Cat. I owed it to Grizabella, and I owed it to that sweet lady on the train who had only wanted a friend to keep her company for a couple hours.

CHAPTER TWENTY

THREE WEEKS LATER

After a quiet Thanksgiving at home, life returned to its usual insanity. Nan crafted a custom advent calendar, which guided us through a series of over-the-top holiday festivities. A simple trip to get the pets' photos taken with Santa Claus had somehow managed to turn into a fresh murder investigation, and it was honestly even crazier than the one we'd looked into on the train.

Despite that little hiccough, Nan kept Octo-Cat, Paisley, and me busy practically every second of every day, and for that, I was incredibly appreciative. She was my nan, my favorite person in the whole wide world, and whatever the circumstances that had brought us together, I would always be grateful to have her in my life.

Yes, my little corner of the world had grown by leaps and bounds, but Nan would always be my original number one. That was one thing I knew could never change.

"Quick, quick!" Octo-Cat, a close number two, cried as he scratched at the door to my personal library, begging to be let in. "We won't have much time before she makes us celebrate again."

I laughed when he shuddered at the word celebrate as if it were the filthiest curse word he could possibly imagine.

Once inside the library, I booted up my laptop and logged into my Instagram account. Octo-Cat had begged for his own account, but as his parent and someone who wanted to protect our secret, I had insisted he use mine instead.

"My love!" he cried when a brand-new photo of Grizabella popped into our feed.

She wore a Santa hat and an enormous scowl on her flat feline face. Peak cat.

Octo-Cat purred and rubbed his side against my computer screen, which is precisely the reason we no longer used his iPad to access Instagram. He couldn't help but snuggle her image, but always threw a fit when doing so accidentally booted him from the app.

I clicked heart on the photo and sat back in my seat. I knew this could take a while based on past experience. "Well, what would you like us to comment on this one?" I pressed when he did little more than purr and rub up against the screen for a solid five minutes.

"Tell her she's beautiful and I love her and miss her and cannot wait until fate brings us together again," he gushed, pausing briefly to actually look at the photo before he resumed all the rubbing.

I groaned at the melodrama but complied—very thankful I'd made my profile private. I was also thankful that I knew for a fact Grizabella's new owner read all the comments to her. Otherwise I would never agree to be these two lovebirds' go-between.

Still, no matter how embarrassing this all was for me, I loved how happy it made them both to keep up their long-distance relationship. Sometimes they even video-chatted and took naps together. It was super sweet, actually.

As for that new owner?

She was a friend of Rhonda's from the show cat circle. Christine. And even though they hadn't been close outside of the competitions, they'd always made sure to grab a meal together whenever they wound up in the same town—and that was as good as any friend poor, lonely Rhonda ever had.

Christine was a good one, though. She loved cats every bit as much as Rhonda had, which meant that Grizabella now had a host of new sisters, also award-winning show Himalayans.

Unfortunately, the injury Grizabella had sustained when Jamison threw her in their fight meant that her show days were over, but even though I knew she'd never admit it, I suspected Grizabella was happy to retire and live out the rest of her days as a well-loved pet and a very minor Instagram influencer.

I typed the comment: Octavius says, "She's beautiful and he loves her and misses her and cannot wait until fate brings them together again."

Christine and everyone else thought I was just being an overly dramatic pet owner with these comments, and I was happy to let them believe that. After all, I really did love my cat bunches.

Right after I pushed enter, the doorbell chimed to the tune of "Memories" from the Broadway show Cats. I hadn't realized Grizabella was named for the play, but Nan made the connection immediately and made sure we mixed in plenty of Andrew Lloyd Weber scores to complement our constant string of Christmas carols.

"I'll be right back," I told the swoony tabby.

He didn't even acknowledge me as I dismissed myself, such was the enormity of a new photo from his lady love—even though we got at least one of them every single day. Young love, adorable.

"Coming!" I called as I bounded down the stairs. The stained-glass windows that hung on either side of the entryway cast rainbow shapes against the hardwood floor but did not reveal the identity of the person waiting on the porch.

When I flung the door open, an unfamiliar young woman stood waiting with a suitcase at her side.

"Cousin!" she cried and reached out to hug me.

I awkwardly accepted her embrace, and upon pulling away, I realized that I did recognize her.

Mostly because her face was almost an exact replica of mine. We were also both tall and curvy. The most noticeable differences between us were the fact that her hair was so blonde it was almost white while mine took on more of a sandy brown hue. Also, I wore an awesome 80s inspired outfit while she sported a prim cardigan buttoned up to the neck and a flowing peasant skirt that reached down to her ankles. A giant gold filigree locket hung halfway down her chest, reminding me of Rhonda's heirloom necklace.

She bit her lip as she studied me, then started to panic, her skin turning bright red as she did. "Oh, no. You are Angie, aren't you? Oh my gosh. If you're not, I'm so embarrassed right now."

"I am Angie," I said with a friendly smile. "I just didn't realize anyone was coming."

"My aunt told your nan and... Let me guess, she didn't relay the message?"

"Sounds like your aunt and my nan have a lot in common," I said with a laugh. "Please, please come in."

I took her suitcase and set it by the stairs, then guided her to the kitchen in search of snacks. Snacks made everything better, especially Nan's homemade baked goods.

My cousin accepted a bottle of Evian and twisted the cap off at once. "You must have gotten quite the shock. I'm sorry nobody told you I'd be coming for the rest of the year."

This made me pause in my search. "The rest of the year?"

"Well, I mean it's just a couple more weeks, right? Sixteen days total, actually, just like you were supposed to have for your trip to Larkhaven. I couldn't wait to meet you, so Aunt Linda suggested I come to you instead. Only I flew instead of taking the train. I mean, who would want to take a train when there are so many faster ways to travel these days?" She giggled and made a funny face. If I hadn't already decided I liked her, that would have definitely done the trick.

I laughed again as I handed my guest one of the chocolate chip banana muffins that Nan had baked just yesterday. "Well, I may not have known you were coming, but I'm really happy you're here. This may be a teensy bit awkward, but… Um, what's your name?"

"Oh, gosh! Sorry! Mags McAllister here," she said, hugging me tight again and speaking around a mouth full of muffin. "Your long-lost cousin from Larkhaven, Georgia, and I can already tell that we're going to get along just great!"

Warmth spread through me as I relaxed into her embrace.

I'd never had a sister, brother, or cousin with Mom being an only child—a fact I constantly bemoaned growing up. But now with Mags here, I sensed how important this new cousin would become to me.

And even though I didn't quite know it yet, the next couple weeks would show just how important, indeed.

WHAT'S NEXT?

Nobody does the holidays like small-town Maine, and my particular small town just so happens to be the very best at decking the halls and rocking around the big Christmas tree downtown.

Yes, every year, Glendale puts on a Holiday Spectacular that's grander and greater than the one that came before. Unfortunately, the only thing everyone's going to remember this year is the two dead bodies that show up in the center of the ice sculpture garden.

With the whole town having come out to play, everyone's in close proximity to the crime scene—and everyone's a suspect. A great many fingers are pointed my way, too, since it was me and my cat that discovered the deathly duo. With only my whacky Nan, recently discovered cousin, overly optimistic Chihuahua, and snarky feline to help me, can I clear my name and save Christmas all in one perfectly executed investigation?

Hold on to your jingle bells, because it's going to be a wild ride.

Pre-order to save! HOPPY HOLIDAY HOMICIDE is just $2.99 until it releases on December 12.

Get your copy here!
mollymysteries.com/HoppyHolidayH

SNEAK PEEK: HOPPY HOLIDAY HOMICIDE

Hi. I'm Angie Russo, and while you may not immediately recognize it, I'm probably one of the most unusual people you'll ever meet.

Why?

Well, how many other people do you know who can communicate with animals? And, no, I'm not talking meows, woofs, and chirps. We have actual conversations, and we even solve crimes together—but I'm getting ahead of myself here.

Before I say any more—*shhh!*—my strange ability is a secret that must be protected at all costs. Not because I'm in danger or anything, just because I'd rather people not know.

Okay?

And, no, I'm not a witch, werewolf, or other kind of fictional supernatural creature. I'm just a normal girl in her late twenties who got electrocuted by an old coffee maker and woke up with the power to communicate with animals.

First, it was just the one cat, Octo-Cat as I call him. He was in the room when I got zapped. We were both there for a will reading, me as the lowly paralegal and him as the primary beneficiary.

When he realized I could understand him, he revealed that his late owner had been murdered even though everyone thought the rich old lady had died of natural causes. Turns out that wasn't what had happened at all.

She'd been murdered, and now he needed me to help him prove it.

Well, we got justice for Ethel Fulton and eventually wound up living in her stately manor home. Since none of the relatives wanted Octo-Cat and I really, really wanted him, we ended up together, too.

We live with my eccentric grandmother, who's known around these parts simply as Nan. A few months ago, we also adopted a rescue Chihuahua named Paisley. She's the sugar to Octo-Cat's spice, and the cute little thing can never say a bad word about anyone…

Well, except for about the naughty raccoon named Pringle who lives in our backyard. He used to live under the porch, but then he kind of blackmailed us into building him a custom treehouse—two treehouses, actually. Oh, boy, is that a long story.

Speaking of long stories, I've got several of those. Just you wait.

You see, a lot has changed in the months since Octo-Cat and I officially opened our P.I. business together. We haven't had a single paying client yet, but we're still getting tons of experience by accidentally stumbling into one mystery after the next.

Hey, whatever works. Right?

Oh, also, I'm in love with my boyfriend and former boss, Charles Longfellow, III—although I haven't exactly told him that yet.

Octo-Cat is also in a long-distance relationship with a former show cat and minor Instagram influencer named Grizabella. And he never stops telling her—or anyone who will listen—just how much he loves her. He's even started giving me guff about how slow Charles and I are moving by comparison.

Then there's the fact that we've discovered Nan isn't actually biologically related to me or my mom, but we're still working on digging up the full story there. Yes, this entire time, she hasn't understood the reason we were shoved together, either.

On the positive side of that crazy bit of news, we have connected with long-lost family in Larkhaven, Georgia. I was supposed to visit them last month, but a murder derailed our travel plans just a bit. So, instead, my cousin Mags showed up here and is staying through the end of the month.

Mags is a hoot, and we all love her. She and I have so much in common and look so much alike that I sometimes wonder if we're not actually twins instead of just cousins.

She's a couple years older than me, though, and as far as I can tell, she's completely normal. Her family owns a candle shop in her town's historic district, and she's promised to teach Nan and me how to make our own candles before she heads back home.

We have lots to do before that happens, though.

For one thing, it's almost Christmas. Nan keeps all of us busy with the custom advent calendar she made at one of her community art classes, and today we're also scheduled to head into town for the twelfth annual Holiday Spectacular!

The Holiday Spectacular is a time-honored tradition for our small town of Glendale. People come from all over Blueberry Bay to gather around the big tree downtown, compete in the ice sculpture competition, and celebrate Christmas with the staggering variety of small businesses downtown.

We get everything from hot cocoa stations to learning Christmas carols from around the world to meeting local authors and getting signed books from them to…

Well, each year is completely different, and that's what makes it so much fun. I can't wait to show Mags my hometown at its best. I hope she'll love it every bit as much as I do.

Hey, look at that, it's time to go find out!

I smacked my lips together after dragging my new cranberry red lip stain across them. Perfect for the holidays. Normally, I wore very little makeup, since my clothes made enough of a statement without any outside help. Lately, though, Nan had begun insisting I put a little more effort into my appearance. She claimed it was for all the holiday festivities, but I suspected she secretly hoped that my glamorous new efforts might rub off on my cousin, Mags.

It's not that Mags was plain, but she did prefer a simple, non-fussy wardrobe. While working in her family's candle shop in the historic district, she actually wore old-fashioned clothing with big skirts and a bonnet—and I suspected that was all the fuss she could handle. I didn't blame her for wanting to keep it easy during her leisure time.

Mags's signature knock sounded at my

bedroom door—three short, one long, two short again.

"Come in!" I called, turning away from the mirror and toward the door.

Mags wore a white button-down shirt and white skirt with white flats. Her white-blonde hair fell midway down her waist, and her fair skin had not a stitch of makeup on it. She looked like a snow angel... or a ghost.

"Can I borrow an outfit from you today?" she asked with a frown. "I think I'm letting Nan down with my color choices."

I laughed. "Don't worry about Nan. I let her down constantly. She still loves us both, though."

"She offered to let me wear something from her wardrobe, but Angie—" Mags dropped her voice to a whisper and motioned for me to lean closer. "Everything's hot pink!"

We broke apart in giggles.

"Seriously, though, please help a cousin out," she begged, joining her hands in front of her and shaking them at me.

I skipped toward the closet, loving every minute of having my long-lost cousin here. I couldn't believe we had less than a week left together. I was going to miss her so much when she went back home.

"How's this?" I asked, tossing a Santa-print party dress at her. It was the same one I'd worn when we took the pets to get their pictures done with Santa at the pet shop in Dewdrop Springs. While it was one of my favorites, I had tons of holiday wear that hadn't made it out of the closet yet this year.

That was the thing about doing most of my shopping at Good Will: everything was so cheap and went toward a good cause, so I had zero issue indulging my addiction. Today I wore a pair of jeans with the ugliest Christmas sweater I owned—it had giant pom-poms stuck in a huge ring to form a three-dimensional Christmas wreath, complete with jingle bells and a giant satin ribbon.

It was wretched, and I adored it.

"This is perfect," Mags said after a quick appraisal of the dress.

"Goes good with pigtails," I said.

She turned crimson. "I think that's perhaps a little too much for today."

Octo-Cat trotted in with Paisley following close behind.

"Mommy, you look gorgeous!" the Chihuahua cried.

"One day that sweater will be mine," my tabby swore. "You can't tell me that's not meant to be a cat toy. Look at all those mischievous floofs!"

Well, he had me there.

"Mommy, can I come, too?" Paisley asked, her tail wagging so fast that it was little more than a black blur.

"She can't talk to us in front of Mags, genius," Octo-Cat said, looking bored with the whole thing.

Mags smiled at me, probably wondering why I had suddenly stopped talking when the animals entered. Let's just say it was incredibly hard to keep my secret from her, especially considering she was family. Still, the fewer people who knew, the better. And I didn't know if she would even believe me. I didn't want to send her screaming back to Georgia and ruin our relationship with the rest of the family before we even got the chance to meet them.

Just one more week to go. I could keep my secret for that long…

Um, right?

Pre-order to save! HOPPY HOLIDAY HOMICIDE is just $2.99 until it releases on December 12.

Get your copy here!
mollymysteries.com/HoppyHolidayH

WHAT'S AFTER THAT?

A new year means a new mayor in the sleepy seaside town of Glendale. Unfortunately, not everyone's happy about his election. In fact, someone's so unhappy that they kidnap his beloved golden retriever and leave a ransom note claiming they'll only return the dog when the man resigns his position.

Enter Angie and Octo-Cat with their first official paying case. Little does the mayor know that while they work to safely recover his ransomed retriever, they'll also be investigating his past to figure out why someone would go so far to keep him out of office.

Can a talking cat find a missing dog? Will

he even want to? Find out in the latest adventure of Pet Whisperer P.I.

Pre-order to save! RETRIEVER RANSOM is just $2.99 until it releases on January 15.

Get your copy here! mollymysteries.com/RetrieverR

MORE FROM BLUEBERRY BAY

Welcome to Blueberry Bay, a scenic region of Maine peppered with quaint small towns and home to a shocking number of mysteries. If you loved this book, then make sure to check out its sister series from other talented Cozy Mystery authors…

Pet Whisperer P.I.
By Molly Fitz

Glendale is home to Blueberry Bay's first ever talking cat detective. Along with his ragtag gang of human and animal helpers, Octo-Cat is determined to save the day… so long as it doesn't interfere with his schedule. Start with

book one, *Kitty Confidential*, which is now available to buy or borrow!
Visit www.MollyMysteries.com for more.

Little Dog Diner
By Emmie Lyn

Misty Harbor boasts the best lobster rolls in all of Blueberry Bay. There's another thing that's always on the menu, too. Murder! Dani and her little terrier, Pip, have a knack for being in the wrong place at the wrong time... which often lands them smack in the middle of a fresh, new murder mystery and in the crosshairs of one cunning criminal after the next. Start with book one, *Mixing Up Murder*, which is now available to buy or borrow!
Visit www.EmmieLynBooks.com for more.

Shelf Indulgence
By S.E. Babin

Dewdrop Springs is home to Tattered Pages, a popular bookshop specializing in rare editions, a grumpy Persian cat named Poppy, and some of the most suspicious characters you'll ever meet. And poor Dakota Adair has just inherited it all. She'll need to make peace with her new cat and use all her book smarts to catch a killer or she might be the next to wind up dead in the stacks. Start with book one, *Hardback Homicide*, which is now available to buy or borrow! Visit www.SEbabin.com for more.

Haunted Housekeeping
By R.A. Muth

Cooper's Cove is home to Blueberry Bay's premier estate cleaning service. Tori and Hazel, the ill-fated proprietors of Bubbles and Troubles, are prepared to uncover a few skeletons. But when a real one turns up, they'll have to solve the mystery quickly if they're going to save their reputations--and their lives. Book one, *The Squeaky Clean Skeleton,* will be coming soon. Keep an eye on www.QuirkyCozy.com for more.

The Cursed Cat of Caraway
By F.M. Storm

Quiet, secluded, and most importantly, far away from his annoying magical family, Guy couldn't wait to start a new life on Caraway Island. Unfortunately, he hadn't counted on his four-year-old daughter coming into her own witchy powers early… or on her accidentally murdering one of the PTO moms. Oops! Book one, *The Kindergarten Coven,* will be coming soon. Keep an eye on www.QuirkyCozy.com for more.

MORE MAGS!

Mags McAllister enjoys her work as a candlestick maker in the historic district of Larkhaven, Georgia—never asking for anything more from her simple life. Then, one day, a white cat with mismatched eyes shows up outside her shop and refuses to leave—not for rain, not for tourists, not for anything.

Mags reluctantly takes him home, only to find that his presence changes everything inside her echoing plantation-style home. Nothing looks changed, but whenever Shadow is near, she can hear voices and sounds that shouldn't be there. Even worse, the next time she enters her family's candle shop, she meets a disembodied voice who shares her name and claims Mags will also share her fate if they can't solve the mystery that's haunted this location since 1781… and quickly, because she won't be able to maintain her strength for long.

Talk about a cold case!

Can the twenty-first-century Mags finally free her eighteenth-century counterpart, or has Shadow just signed her death warrant by opening her ears to the supernatural secrets that surround her normally sleepy small town?

To be notified when SECRETS OF THE SPECTER (the first in Mag's new series) goes live, make sure you sign up for Molly's newsletter at mollymysteries.com/subscribe

You definitely don't want to miss what happens next!

ABOUT MOLLY FITZ

While USA Today bestselling author Molly Fitz can't technically talk to animals, she and her doggie best friend, Sky Princess, have deep and very animated conversations as they navigate their days. Add to that, five more dogs, a snarky feline, comedian husband, and diva daughter, and you can pretty much imagine how life looks at the Casa de Fitz.

Molly lives in a house on a high hill in the Michigan woods and occasionally ventures out for good food, great coffee, or to meet new animal friends.

Writing her quirky, cozy animal mysteries is pretty much a dream come true, but she also goes by the name Melissa Storm (also a USA Today bestselling author, yay!) and writes a very different kind of story.

Learn more, grab the free app, or sign up for her newsletter at www.MollyMysteries.com!

MORE FROM MOLLY

If you're ready to dive right in to more Pet Whisperer P.I., then you can even order the other books right now by clicking below:

Kitty Confidential

Terrier Transgressions

Hairless Harassment

Dog-Eared Delinquent

The Cat Caper

Chihuahua Conspiracy

Raccoon Racketeer

Himalayan Hazard

Hoppy Holiday Homicide

Retriever Ransom

Lawless Litter

Legal Seagull

Pet Whisperer P.I. Books 1-3

Six Merry Little Murders

CONNECT WITH MOLLY

Sign up for Molly's newsletter for book updates and cat pics:
mollymysteries.com/subscribe

Download Molly's app for cool bonus content:
mollymysteries.com/app

Join Molly's reader group on Facebook to make new friends: **mollymysteries.com/group**

Made in the USA
Columbia, SC
16 April 2021